BLURRED LINES

THE TIES THAT BIND BOOK 2

KL RAMSEY

Blurred Lines Copyright © 2019 by K.L. Ramsey.

Cover design Copyright © 2019 by miblart

Imprint:Independently published

First Print Edition: June 2019

All rights reserved.

No part of this book may be reproduced, scanned, or distributed in any printed or electronic form without permission. Please do not participate in or encourage piracy of copyrighted materials in violation of the author's rights. Thank you for respecting the hard work of this author.

This is a work of fiction. Names, characters, places, and incidents either are the product of the author's imagination or are used fictitiously, and any resemblance to locales, events, business establishments, or actual persons—living or dead—is entirely coincidental.

ANTON

Anton Rossi paced the alleyway outside the small warehouse. What he was about to do would cross all the fucking lines but he didn't care anymore. He lived with so many blurred lines already, what was a few more gray areas? He was about done with waiting though and if Luca didn't come back out of the fucking warehouse in the next two minutes, he was going in after him.

Anton was sure Luca Gallo was the sexiest man he had ever met and he was doubly sure he was pure trouble. Besides his last name being Gallo, he had the reputation for being a complete bad-ass with a total disregard for any rules he didn't feel like following. He was the great nephew of Anthony Gallo Sr. and while that fact alone should warrant him a secure position in the Gallo organization, his inability to follow rules usually knocked him down a few pegs. And now, Anton was saddled with babysitting the sexy as sin man who for all rights and purposes should be his senior. His problem was he had a thing for men who were a little older than him and besides having that going for him, Luca was Anton's walking wet dream. He was the biggest man Anton had ever seen. They had often spent early mornings working out together and strong didn't even begin to describe Luca's abilities. He was a mountain of muscles and a complete turn-on, with all his tattoos and dark hair. His crystal blue eyes haunted Anton's dreams. Every time Luca looked at him it was as if he could see straight through to Anton's soul and that thought made him both hot and uncomfortable at the same time.

Anton never told anyone about being bisexual, not even the two people he was closest to—his mother and sister. The thought of "coming out" scared the shit out of him. It was a part of who he was but sharing that side of himself with anyone else felt foreign. He hoped someday he could live with that part of himself openly. For now, that wasn't an option for him, so he kept his longing for Luca and that piece of himself a secret.

Luca came barreling out of the back entrance of the warehouse holding up two tickets and smiling like a lunatic. Anton couldn't help but return his smile, it was infectious. "I got us two front row seats to the show tonight," he shouted. Anton grabbed Luca's arm and lowered it so he could take the tickets from him. They were their guarantee they'd be front row center for the largest auction of women in the area. They were also just what he needed to help with his plan to bring down the Marino family's human trafficking ring, earning him points with both Isabella Gallo and his detective brother-in-law, Nick James. Sure, playing both sides was a dangerous game but for now it was all he had. Isabella Gallo wouldn't know what hit her once he turned over the evidence he was compiling on the Gallo family. If Anton could bring down a few other families, like the Marinos, that would be a bonus. He had been working with his brother-in-law for almost a year now and he knew sooner or later, he'd find exactly what Nick needed to bring down the whole fucking Gallo organization.

"You can't go waving these things around Luca," Anton chided. Luca smiled and shrugged and God help him Anton's heart raced just from the sight of how beautiful the man was.

"Well, I guess I got a little excited," Luca said. "I've been going in there for months now, begging for two fucking tickets and they chose today to give them to me. I felt like it was Christmas morning and my birthday all wrapped up in one pretty box." Anton laughed at Luca's analogy. It was pretty fucking lucky they finally scored tickets to the auction, but he was a little suspicious as to why now? Luca was right, he had been going into that warehouse for months. They both had and all the sudden, today is their lucky day?

"Ani, you have that look again." Luca flashed him a wolfish grin that instantly made him hard. No one except his Ma and Valentine had ever called him Ani. He liked the way Luca used his familiar nickname.

"What look is that, Luca?" He took a step towards the giant man and loved the way Luca's breath hitched. A part of him wanted to believe it was due to the same desire he felt, but he didn't want to get his hopes up. There had been subtle hints Luca might have some feelings towards Anton, but he always brushed them off as the two of them being close friends. They never really discussed their sexuality and Anton wasn't about to start now. He knew Luca liked women but that really didn't mean anything—he did too.

"The look you are worried about something," Luca said, taking a step towards Anton. Their bodies were almost touching and Anton couldn't help the way his traitorous body leaned into Luca's craving more.

"Everything is fine, Luca," Anton lied. He was tall, at six-two, but Luca had at least three more inches on him, causing him to have to look up to see his gorgeous blue eyes. Those eyes told Anton everything he needed to know—Luca didn't believe a fucking word he was saying.

"Sure, nothing to worry about," Luca whispered. His big hand gently brushed Anton's and he knew he should pull his away but he just couldn't bring himself to do it. The connection, the sparks, the desire, from just one touch was almost too much.

"We shouldn't do this here," Anton whispered. Their mouths were mere inches from each other. It would be so easy to lean completely into Luca's body and take what he had been needing from him, but that would be a mistake. The Marino family had eyes and ears everywhere. If Isabella got wind of any kind of relationship between the two men she'd separate them, permanently. The thought of not working with Luca every day, not being with him, wasn't one Anton wanted to entertain.

"Why won't you just let me in, Ani? Why do you keep pushing me away?" Anton shrugged and took a step back breaking their contact. Luca's frustrated groan filled the empty alleyway and Anton shushed him.

"We aren't alone, Luca," Anton warned. "The Marinos have eyes everywhere. This is not the time or place for what is possibly going on between the two of us," Anton barked. He looked Luca up and down searching for some sign he might agree something was happening between them.

Luca smiled, "So, there is something then?" Anton didn't make a move to answer, afraid to admit he desperately wanted the man standing in front of him. He hated feeling this unsure about himself, it wasn't who he was. He was usually confident to the point of being cocky, it's what got him through most situations. Even Isabella Gallo wasn't immune to his charms but Luca was another story.

"Anton, tell me there is something," Luca demanded, crowding into his personal space again. Anton nodded, not trusting his own voice. Luca pushed Anton's body against the brick building pressing his own body against his and dipped down to take Anton's lips in a hard scorching kiss. All the pent- up desire

Anton had let build up over the past few months came boiling to the surface and he couldn't get enough of Luca. He rubbed his erection against Luca's big thigh wanting so much more than he could take while they were in the public eye.

Luca broke the kiss leaving them both breathless. "That's so much fucking better," Luca growled. "I've wanted to do that for months, Ani." The big guy had the audacity to wink at him—which was totally his move—and walk back to their car, sliding into the driver's seat.

"I take it you're driving then?" Anton called after him. Luca's sexy smirk said it all—he liked being in the driver's seat.

"Get used to it," Luca teased and slammed his door. Yeah, playing with Luca Gallo was dangerous but Anton was pretty sure it was going to be a hell of a lot of fun too.

SOFIA

Sofia Marino sat in her little room off the main stage the guys called the "show room". It was disgusting really; a place for them to show off their new goods available for sale to the highest bidders. Unfortunately for her, the goods they dealt with were women they planned to sell into slavery. She knew her fate but waiting her turn was excruciating. Most of the girls had been brought in from other states and even other countries and were there for the sole purpose of being sold off to the highest bidder. What happened to them after that was up to their new owner. The thought of being a slave to a fat, old man, whose only way to get a woman was to buy her, made Sofia sick. She would rather die before she let herself be taken by one of those pigs.

"Hey Princess," one of the guards teased her, carrying in a tray of food. "Lunch is served." She had been refusing to eat since they threw her into the room a day and a half ago. Honestly, she was starving and would eat just about anything, but refusing food seemed to piss off her captors. Sofia reveled in their anger, loving the way she seemed to get under their skin made her happy. It was the only happiness she had now.

"You might as well just take it with you. I won't eat that," she whispered. She grabbed the bottled water from the tray, tormenting herself with the smell of the food and turned to sit back down on her bed.

"Suit yourself, but I have a feeling you're going to want to eat this, Princess. Tonight is a big night for you and well, one of our lucky bidders. You're going to be the main attraction. Our very own mafia virgin." He dropped the tray on the bedside table and turned to leave her tiny room, chuckling at his own words.

Telling her captors she was a virgin had not been her best idea. When they brought her in she panicked when four guards were talking about testing her out before they put her up for auction. So, she blurted out she was a virgin, which wasn't a lie—she was. They seemed even more turned on by her truth, but then another man walked into the small room where they had stripped her bare to inspect her body and told the four goons to leave her alone. Since then, no one has laid so much as a finger on her and she was thankful for that. Now, she was beginning to see her truth won her top billing at the auction. Apparently, men loved a virgin and would pay extra for one—a whole lot extra. The thought made her sick.

Sofia had been saving herself for the right man,

someone she knew loved her. Hell, at just twenty-one, she thought she had plenty of time to find the right guy, fall in love and have the whole dream. But that fantasy was all gone. Tonight, she would be sold off to some guy and he would get to take her virginity. She needed a plan but every one she came up with ended with her taking her own life. At least she wouldn't belong to anyone then. She'd be free and it would be on her own terms, so that had to count for something.

She stood and crossed the small room to where her guard had set her tray. Sofia eyed the offensive plate of food and realized the big goon was right. If she was going to be sold off tonight she would need her strength —every ounce of it. She wouldn't go down without a fight and she sure in hell wouldn't let some old, disgusting, pervert take her virginity without getting a few jabs in. Then she'd either find a way to escape or end it all. The thought had her smiling and she picked up the plate of food.

Sofia shoveled pasta into her mouth by the fork full and groaned at just how good it tasted. She was so hungry; she would have eaten just about anything, but this was actually good. Sofia stood by the only window in her room and looked down at the street below. She was about three stories up and the metal bars on the small window wouldn't budge. She tried that route of escape her first night but there was no way out. Sofia was smart enough to realize there would be no rescue, she was entirely alone without any hope of freedom.

She watched two men down below by the

warehouse back entrance and thought the one guy had to be the biggest she had ever seen. He was talking to another man who was dressed in a dark suit with his black hair slicked back. He reminded Sofia of so many of her father's friends—well, former friends. He had mafia written all over him. The two were talking so closely she was sure they were going to start making out any moment. She held her breath anticipating the kiss she was sure would happen but the man in the dark suit backed away. Sofia took another bite of pasta and nearly choked when the larger man pushed the man in the suit against the brick wall and kissed him.

Sofia couldn't look away from them, everything about the kiss was raw with passion. She felt like an intruder but she wanted to see more, hell—she wanted to be more than just a spectator. Her cheeks warmed as did most of her other girl parts and she was pretty sure she was blushing. When the kiss was over, they got into their black SUV and left. Sofia stood there by her window wondering who the two men were. If they worked for the Marino family, she hadn't seen them before. She knew most of the men in the family due to her father's service to the Marinos. She didn't recognize them, she was sure she would have remembered the two of them.

Her father, Vincent Marino was a boss in the Marino organization but that all changed when he defied orders, going against the head of the family. It was a death sentence for him but the family didn't stop there. She and her mother were both disgraced and marked as traitors even though she had no idea what sin her father committed. A few days ago, Sofia was leaving her apartment to go to the gym when two of the family's goons forced her into the back of their SUV. She thought for sure they were going to kill her like they did her father months prior but what they had planned for her was much worse.

They had kept her locked up in the tiny room for almost two days now and she worried she might never find her way out or back home to her mother. Hell, she didn't even know if her mother was alive or if she would even have a home to go to. She finished her food and shoved the tray aside.

"Good job, Princess," another guard came into her room to retrieve her tray. This one was always a little nicer to her than the first guy. She hated the way they both called her Princess though. It was a term reserved for the boss's daughters but she wasn't that person anymore, not since they killed her father.

"I didn't do it for you, asshole," she growled. The guard laughed and hung a white dress in her closet.

"You need to take a shower and be in this dress by six," he commanded.

"And if I refuse?" she countered, raising her chin in defiance.

"Well, we have your sweet mother just down the hall. We've been given orders not to touch either of you unless you refuse to cooperate. I know your mother isn't a virgin but I'm betting she's a lot of fun," he threatened. She gasped at the thought of them holding her mother captive or someone putting their hands on her.

"Yeah, now you're getting it. So, do yourself and your pretty Ma a favor and just do what I fucking tell you to do, Princess." He picked up her tray and left the room.

Sofia walked over to the closet and pulled out the white dress that reminded her of a wedding gown. "Of course," she whispered, "A virgin bride." She threw the dress onto her bed and went into the small, adjoining bathroom to shower, as instructed. Sofia had no choice, she would have to play their game but when and if she saw her chance to escape, she would. Even if taking her own life was the only way to break free, she'd do it. Death was a better alternative than living as a slave. In fact, if those were her only choices, she'd prefer it that way.

LUCA

Luca stepped out of the shower and wrapped a towel around his waist. He needed to get his shit together and be ready in the next ten minutes when Anton was due to pick him up for the auction. He was looking forward to the night out with his sexy partner, but he hated they were going there on business. Honestly, he found the whole idea of auctioning off women to the highest bidder barbaric. He wasn't sure if he could tell Ani that though since his partner was basically the right hand man to the head of the Gallo family. There was no way he wanted to piss off Isabella Gallo again, already being on thin ice with the matriarch. Luca was trying, really trying to do as told, but he hated all the damn rules that made his life feel like a fucking prison sentence.

His great uncle was the head of the Gallo family until his death. Everyone thought his son, Anthony Jr., had taken over as head of the family but they were wrong. Isabella had taken the reins and she had a tight grip on them, making sure her three sons didn't double cross her and try to push her out. He had to hand it to her, she was a force to be reckoned with. Luca just liked being a spectator when it came to watching Isabella lower the hammer and not the one on the receiving end of the blow. He slipped up a few times, deciding to play by his own rules instead of Isabella's and he paid for his mistakes. Now, he was stuck being babysat by her right hand guy and that sucked. Anton was seven years his junior and for all intents should be his underling. Luca had to admit, if he had to have a babysitter, Anton Rossi wasn't bad to have watching over him. He knew that Ani would always have his back and after the events of that afternoon—the scorching kiss they shared—hopefully he'd have his front too.

Luca heard the pounding on his front door and smiled knowing it was Ani. He pulled on his pants and ran down the steps to let Anton into his town home. He threw the door open to find Ani standing on the other side, his dark hair slicked back from his shower and his soulful brown eyes intensely taking in every inch of Luca's bare torso. He liked the way Ani shamelessly let his eyes roam his body and hoped like hell he was as turned on by the electricity Luca felt between them every time they were in the same room together. Luca had always liked both men and women, although he didn't really date a whole lot of men. It was easier to be with women, especially in a mafia family. Chicago was a big city, but when it came to being part of a mafia family, it was like living under a fucking microscope. Everyone knew everyone else's business. He had been with a few men but chose to keep his relationships with them on the down low, not wanting any extra flack over his sexual preferences. Besides, whom he dated was his concern and no one else's.

"Hmm," Anton hummed. "Not ready yet I see," he said, more amused than angry. "How long will it take you to get ready, Princess? I'd like to get front row seats tonight and you are going to ruin that for me, aren't you?" Ani teased. He pushed past him, letting himself into Luca's home. He had been there a few times, mostly to pick Luca up for a job but occasionally he came over to catch a game.

"I'm not going to make you late for your night at the meat market," he grumbled. Luca noticed the way Anton winced at his statement and he wondered if he felt the same way about having to watch women being sold to the highest bidder. The whole idea made Luca sick, but it was part of his job and part of the world he was born into.

"Just keep in mind tonight is about business," Anton reminded. "We aren't there to bid on any women, just get intel on the Marino family to report back to Isabella."

Luca nodded, "Right, no women," he teasingly agreed. "Any other orders, sir?" he asked. Anton didn't look as amused by Luca's teasing. He seemed a little out of sorts and Luca wondered if it was because Anton was nervous about tonight or about their kiss earlier.

They had known each other for a while now but today was a new twist in their relationship and he hoped they didn't cross a line that would make working together awkward.

"What's up, Ani?" Luca took a step towards him closing the space between them. "You know you can tell me anything, right?" Luca questioned. God, he meant it. He wanted Anton to let him in, but he knew Ani had walls built up all around him and it would take a fucking wrecking ball to tear them down. Still, Luca wanted to try. He reached out and laid a hand on Ani's arm needing the contact but truthfully wanting to see if he'd have the same reaction as earlier.

"Those damn sparks," Anton whispered.

"Thank fuck," Luca growled. "You feel them too?" he asked. Anton nodded and Luca thought his heart would beat out of his chest.

"What do we do now?" Anton asked. "How do we work together and not blur the lines?"

"Fuck the lines," Luca growled. He pressed his body up against Anton's noting how they seemed to perfectly align, as if they fit together. He kissed his way into Ani's mouth loving his breathy sighs as he licked his way in. Anton took everything he offered and gave so much more in return. Luca's skin felt like it was on fire; almost as if there was an electric current running through his body everywhere Ani touched him. Luca couldn't seem to get enough of him and when Anton broke their kiss, leaving them both panting for air, he could see the raw desire in Ani's eyes.

"As much as I'd like to continue this," Anton said, motioning between their two bodies, "we need to get a move on. We have a job to do first, then we can pick this up later," he promised. Luca smiled at him and nodded knowing when Anton put his mind to something there was no stopping him. Ani wanted to get tonight's job over with, check it off his mental list and then Luca would hopefully be able to convince Anton to spend the night. He just hoped that crossing the line with Anton didn't come back to bite him in the ass.

ANTON

Anton wasn't sure what to do with all the crazy feelings that were consuming him every time he and Luca were in the same room together. He was having trouble keeping his hands and his lips to himself lately when it came to the sexy Italian man. Sure Luca was his type, but there was something more about him and Anton was hoping to see where this thing between them ended up.

They got to the auction early enough to get a front row seat. Anton strategically picked a spot that would allow him to be close enough to the Marino family's table to get the information he needed.

"Wow, this is quite a crowd of who's who here tonight. I think every mob family from Chicago to New York is in the building," Luca whispered. Anton couldn't help his laugh. The big guy wasn't a quiet whisperer and he knew half the room heard Luca.

"You whisper louder than any other human being I've ever met," Anton teased.

Luca shot him a wolfish grin. "Well, nothing about me is average, Ani," he boasted. Anton knew just what Luca was referring to and he couldn't shake the mental image of Luca completely naked from his overly active imagination. A soft moan escaped his parted lips giving away just what he was thinking.

"Yeah, now you're getting it," Luca teased. He threw back his head and his booming laugh filled the room garnering them attention from everyone around them. The last thing they needed was to get thrown out of the place before the auction even began.

"Keep it down," Anton grumbled. "You're going to get us booted out of here and Isabella will be pissed. That's the last thing either of us needs at this point." Luca sobered and nodded. Anton knew his partner had made a few questionable mistakes lately and the Gallo family didn't allow for mishaps. He wanted to make sure Luca stayed on the straight and narrow, otherwise Isabella would take matters into her own hands and things would get nasty. She was ruthless when she felt betrayed. It was as if Isabella had to prove herself worthy not only to her own family but to all the other families in the area. Showing weakness wasn't an option for Isabella Gallo.

Months prior, when she found out Luca was basically making his own rules and going against the Gallo family, Isabella wanted to use his disobedience as an example to the rest of the members. She didn't care if Luca's last name was Gallo, she saw him as her way to make a name for herself. Isabella planned on using Luca to show everyone just how powerful she was but Anton intervened. He had seen the big guy around and even worked with him on a few jobs. He wasn't just physically attracted to Luca—he thought he was a good guy that had just made a few stupid mistakes. Hell, if Isabella knew what Anton was up to, working with his detective brother-in-law to turn evidence, he would have been in the same boat as Luca. So, Anton did what he was good at, he made Isabella a deal she couldn't pass up just like he did when he secured his mother and sister's freedom from the Gallo family.

Anton was good at digging up evidence no one else wanted found. He always had some dirt on someone and he usually held it close to his vest not sharing it until the moment was right. When Isabella saw the evidence he had against the Marino family, he became an asset to her and she would do just about anything to get her hands on all the dirt Ani had. He gave Isabella trickles of evidence, not wanting to give away his whole hand at once. His father had taught him a good poker player never reveals his cards too early in the game. Anton knew the game he was playing was a dangerous one and he held onto his cards, making sure he was in the game for the long haul.

When he gave the last bit of evidence to Isabella, she asked him what he expected in return. She knew Anton was always up for a good barter and would never just willingly hand over information without a promise of something in return. It's how their relationship worked. He asked to take Luca on as one of his guys claiming to need a partner and Isabella agreed. She also made Anton swear he'd keep the giant troublemaker in check and that was proving to be more difficult than he originally thought. Luca Gallo was trouble wrapped up in one sexy ass package and Ani was quickly finding he had his work cut out for him.

"Let's just remember why we are here tonight, please," he reminded. "We are under strict orders to look but not buy." Isabella sent him in to gather information, not to purchase a woman. He knew there would be hell to pay if he and Luca showed up with a bought woman in tow. Isabella would have both of their balls for it.

"That's a shame, Ani," Luca said. "I think it would be fun to find a woman to put between us," he admitted. Anton knew Luca liked women. Hell, he was with a different one every other night. Luca suddenly looked confused; his expression was almost comical. "You do like women, right?"

Anton bit back his smile, "Yeah, I like women too," he admitted. "I'm bi, Luca." Luca breathed a sigh of relief and sat back in his chair. "I assume the same is true about you?" Anton didn't want to admit he was nervous about Luca's answer but he was. He knew firsthand that Luca wanted him. He just wanted to hear him admit it.

"Yes," Luca said. "I am. I have to admit I've thought about you, me and a woman together more times than I care to admit." That thought made Anton hot. He had the same fantasies about Luca, he just never imagined he'd meet someone who shared his same desires and kinks. In a perfect fantasy world Anton would be with a man and a woman. He saw how well it worked for his sister Valentine, but he never imagined he would be able to find what she and her husbands had together.

"Well fuck," Anton swore. He needed to get his unruly cock under control because the show was about to begin. He had to remember why they were there and then he wanted to end up in bed with Luca before the night was over. He really didn't give a shit what anyone else thought anymore. He wanted Luca and if they were careful, no one else would have to know about the two of them—especially not Isabella Gallo.

The commotion backstage told him the auction was about to begin and he was happy for the distraction. The last thing he wanted to do was continue his conversation about he and Luca in bed with a woman. It was almost too much to wrap his brain around right now and he needed to focus his full attention on everyone else around them. He could feel Luca watching him but he pretended not to notice. Anton sat up in his chair waiting for the first woman to appear on stage after the announcement was made the show was about to start.

They watched as countless women stood on stage, mostly naked and crying as they were sold off to the highest bidder. It was hard to watch and nothing about the whole night seemed appealing to Anton. What kind of monster bid on a woman to take home and make into his own personal sex slave? He really hated this whole fucking world but he couldn't just walk away from it. The Gallo family would never let him leave knowing everything he did. He would end up just like his father had and where would that leave his mother and Valentine?

Anton glanced over to find that Luca seemed just as disgusted as he was by the whole scene. He sat next to Anton with his arms crossed over his massive chest and a hateful scowl on his handsome face. By the time they were to the last girl on the docket, Luca looked about ready to murder someone and Anton couldn't say he'd blame him. He felt the same way.

The room almost seemed to hum to life when the auctioneer announced they had a special treat for everyone—a mafia princess virgin bride. The crowd quieted and Anton swore he could hear Luca's heart beating. Luca sat on the edge of his seat as if he was going to launch himself at the stage. A tiny woman dressed in a white gown reluctantly walked down the runway, her chin defiantly raised as if to dare anyone to bid on her. Unlike most of the other girls, she wasn't crying and judging from the pissed off look on her face she was going to give whomever won her a fucking hard time.

"Here we have a true mafia princess, gentlemen. Sofia Marino is our virgin bride and she is sure to please. She is only twenty-one years old and a verified virgin, guaranteed or your money back," the auctioneer promised. Pretty Sofia huffed out her breath and Anton could tell she was full of fight and in a different time and place he might have been interested in her. She was just his type and from the way Luca watched her, she did it for him too.

"Let's start the bidding at five thousand dollars gentlemen," the auctioneer offered. Luca raised his hand, bidding on the sexy mafia princess and Anton didn't hide his frustrated groan.

"What the fuck, man?" Anton questioned. "We aren't here to bid on women, Luca." He was given strict orders not to participate in the bidding by Isabella and he was pretty sure that extended to Luca. She was going to cut their balls off and store them in a jar as a warning to others who dared to disobey her, Anton was sure of it.

"We can't let this happen," Luca spat. "They can't just sell her off like this, it's not right." Anton looked up at the stage where Sofia stood bravely staring down the audience. Her smile was mean and he was pretty sure purchasing her would be a fucking disaster.

"You can't disobey orders, Luca. Isabella will have both of our hides if we waltz through the door with a mafia princess in tow," Anton whispered. Luca flashed him a wolfish grin and he knew there would be no stopping him. One thing he learned about Luca after working so closely with him—if the big guy had his mind set there would be no changing it.

"This isn't about Isabella or family business; this is personal, Ani," Luca whispered. He looked back at the stage and he didn't miss the way Sofia was mean mugging them both. Anton had to admit she was a beauty, but they didn't need the trouble she would cause them. Bidding continued around them and someone at the next table bid eight thousand and Luca shot the guy a look that would have stopped even the most stoic of men in their tracks. Luca was big and he looked menacing when he wanted to.

"How is this personal?" Anton questioned. "And don't tell me this has anything to do with your fucking dick, man," he warned.

Luca laughed and shook his head. "My dick isn't always in control Ani, just ninety percent of the time." Anton shot him a disbelieving look and Luca smiled and winked at him. "Fine, ninety-eight percent of the time." Anton laughed and shook his head.

"Do I hear ten thousand?" the auctioneer shouted. The crowd grew deathly quiet and the auctioneer picked up his gavel to end the sale when Luca raised his hand.

"Ten thousand," he growled.

"Shit," Anton barked. "We're fucking done for, Luca." He didn't seem to give a damn what Anton thought. In fact, he looked damn pleased with himself and Anton wanted to punch the smug grin off Luca's face.

"Sold," the auctioneer yelled over the growing murmur. Anton didn't miss the stares and whispers of the Marino family who sat at the next table. "Please see the man in the back to collect your virgin bride, Sir."

"Let's get her and get the fuck out of here," Anton insisted. "We've attracted the wrong attention and I want to be long gone before this thing goes sideways." Anton wasn't sure how the hell his night went so wrong, so quickly. But his idea of how their night was going to end with him and Luca in bed together just flew out the window. Instead, he and Luca were going to be up late talking about what the hell they were going to do with Sofia Marino—their sexy virgin bride.

SOFIA

Sofia stood on the stage willing herself not to cry. Every time she felt as though her flood gates were going to burst she would bite the inside of her cheeks until she tasted blood. She wouldn't give them that, they didn't deserve to see her tears or know how scared she was. She'd never give them that satisfaction.

When the auctioneer announced her she felt as though she was going to throw up, but then someone pushed her out onto the stage, wearing that fucking hideous white dress and she had no other option than to put on a brave face. She stared down the crowd, paying close attention to the family members sitting front and center. They were her family members—the Marinos who up until recently thought of her as a part of them. Now, since her father went and betrayed them all, she was nothing to them. Actually, she was less than nothing, so easily sold off to the highest bidder.

It was difficult to see into the audience; with the

bright lights they had trained on her. She couldn't really see who was bidding on her but she was sure whomever it was wouldn't matter. She didn't give a shit who had just bought her because she wouldn't stay with him. Her plan to escape fueled her anger and she was ready to fight like hell rather than let some sweaty, bald asshole take her body. Her new owner wouldn't know what hit him and that thought alone was keeping her from giving up hope.

After the bidding was over she was led backstage to wait for whomever purchased her to show up and claim her. Sofia was hoping they would remove the handcuffs so she'd have a fighting chance but the guard shoved her down into a chair and told her not to move.

"Can I get the cuffs off?" she asked the guard.

"No fucking way, Princess," he said. "Not until your new owner gets here to take your sassy ass off my hands." He turned and started talking to another guard and Sofia quickly looked around trying to see if there was a way out of the small hallway. She knew she wouldn't get far in the getup she was forced to wear. The heels were killing her feet and she couldn't wait to slip them off. But, aching feet where probably the least of her problems.

Two guys walked backstage and she noticed they looked familiar. She studied the big one, noting he was probably the largest guy she had ever seen. His muscles looked like they had muscles and he was covered in tattoos making him look the part of mafia boss but he was too young to be one. His dark hair was a little long just the way she liked it but his eyes were what really threw her off. Most Italian guys she knew had brown eyes but this guy had the most striking blue eyes she had ever seen.

The younger guy with him wasn't much smaller than the big guy was and she could tell he was the one in charge. But he was much too young to be high up in any of the families unless he was the son of a boss. They tended to rise in the ranks faster than someone recruited off the streets. The younger guy looked pissed and anxious and she wondered why he was so angry.

They talked to the auctioneer and signed some papers, handing over a wad of cash. "You're up, Princess," the guard growled. He yanked her up by her handcuffs and practically dragged her over to where the two handsome guys were finishing up their business.

"Meet your virgin bride gentlemen," the guard said. He handed Sofia over and the big guy just stood there looking her up and down as if sizing her up. Sofia did the same, looking them both over the way they had her. They were neither bald nor old, as she had imagined they would be. In fact the pair of them were two of the hottest men she had ever seen in her life—not that it mattered. There was no way that she'd let either of them lay a single finger on her body, if she could help it.

"Take off the cuffs," he ordered.

"I think you're going to want to keep them on her," the guard offered.

The big guy smirked at the guard. "I think I can handle her from here," he growled.

"Alright," the guard agreed. He pulled out the key and released Sofia's wrists from the cuffs. She pulled her hands back and rubbed her chafed skin. "It's your funeral, man. But don't say I didn't warn you. If you lose her there are no returns."

"We won't be returning her," the big guy insisted.

The younger guy looked around the room and Sofia followed his gaze realizing why he seemed so nervous. A few of the Marino's guards were closely watching them and she wondered who had just bought her. If she didn't know any better she'd say her old family members seemed a little nervous and she worried they weren't going to let her just walk out of there.

"We need to go," the younger guy barked. He grabbed her wrist tugging her along and Sofia knew if she didn't play nice, she'd be destroying her chances to possibly escape. Staying back at the warehouse and having to live in that tiny cell wasn't her idea of a good time. But leaving with not just one but two men who had just purchased her was more than she bargained for. She might be able to escape one of them but she had a feeling it would be tricky to slip past them both.

The big guy flanked her other side and led her to the closest black SUV. He opened the back door and helped her up into the seat, sliding in beside her. "You drive, Ani," he ordered. The younger guy nodded and rounded the vehicle to get into the driver's seat.

"You're safe now, Sofia," the big guy soothed. He

didn't make a move towards her, not even trying to touch her. She expected him to be all over her, believing that was the reason why he had gotten into the back seat with her but he didn't. He reached across her body and she felt herself holding her breath as if anticipating what he was going to do to her.

"It's alright honey. I just want to fasten your seat belt. My name's Luca by the way. Luca Gallo," he almost whispered.

"So, I've been purchased by the Gallo family? What's the plan here, Luca?" she spat. The guy in the front seat chuckled and Luca shot him a dirty look.

"That's Anton Rossi and we really don't have a plan here," he admitted.

"Well, that sounds great, Luca," she sassed. "So, you two decided to buy me on a whim and what—drive around with me in the back of your car? You know you're probably being followed, right?" she questioned.

Luca looked out the back window as if trying to spot their tail. "She's fucking right, Ani," he growled. He's about four cars back in a black sedan," Luca said.

Anton nodded and sped up, making a sharp right which nearly had her on Luca's lap. He wrapped an arm around her and she wasn't sure what to make of it. It was as if he was trying to protect her rather than cop a feel.

"Don't worry, honey," Luca soothed. "Ani's pretty good at losing a tail."

"After we ditch this guy I think we should head out away from the city for the night. I know of a hotel where we can lay low until we figure out what we are going to do," Anton ordered. "You really fucked up bidding on her, man," he shouted.

Sofia felt as though the two of them seemed familiar but she just couldn't place where she knew either of them from. Chicago was a small city when you grew up in a family. Even though kids didn't mix with other families, they knew each other. They went to school together and hung out at the same popular spots.

"Have we met before?" she asked, looking between the two of them. Anton shook his head, focusing on trying to outrun their tail. She looked back to Luca and his shy smile told her she had guessed correctly.

"Yep," he confirmed grinning like a complete loon. If it wasn't for the fact he had just purchased her at an auction she might actually like the big guy.

"Want to clue me in on how you know me?" she asked. "Did we go to high school together?" she guessed.

Luca snorted and shook his head. "Nope. I'm a bit older than you, honey," he admitted. "You know my younger sister, Mila. You used to come over to our house to play when you were little." Sofia remembered playing over at a girl named Mila's house but that was ages ago. She was only about nine or ten during a time when the Marino and Gallo families had a truce. She remembered Mila's older brother though. She had a giant crush on him and if she was correct, made a complete fool of herself following him around like a lost puppy.

"I remember her," she admitted. "That was so long ago. I hated when our two families started fighting again. I lost so many friends."

"Yeah, me too," Luca sadly admitted.

"I can't believe you remembered me, Luca. You were a teenager then. If I recall correctly, you spent a good deal of your time chasing your poor Ma down begging her to borrow her car," she said.

Luca shyly nodded. "Yeah, that was when we only had one car and I was desperate to get out of that house. There were six of us kids and I was the oldest. I was counting down the seconds until I was old enough to move out of that crowded house." Sofia would have given anything to have a brother or sister. Being an only child was a lonely existence. She used to beg her parents for a sibling but it never happened.

"Guys, I hate to break up your little reunion but I think I lost our tail," Anton said. Luca turned to look out the back window and after a few minutes, he nodded his agreement. "Good. I'll drive around a bit, just to make sure. Then we will head over to the hotel and get some rest. We'll have to figure out what to tell Isabella," Anton grumbled and Sofia wondered who the hell Isabella was.

"Who is Isabella? Are you guys married?" she questioned. Both Luca and Anton barked out their laughs, telling her she had guessed incorrectly.

"No, sweetheart. Isabella Gallo is the head of the family and my boss," Anton said. "We were under orders not to bid tonight but here we are." Anton shot

Luca a disgusted look in the rearview mirror and she wondered what that was all about.

"What are you guys going to do with me?" she whispered. Honestly, she almost didn't want to know but she needed to be prepared for whatever they had planned.

"I'm not sure yet, honey," Luca admitted. "I can't just let you go. The paperwork I signed back there said if I was dissatisfied with the product," he paused and looked her over, "I'm guessing that's you," he continued, "then I'm to return you directly to the Marino family. They weren't kidding about their refund policy. We return you and it's a death sentence for all of us." Sofia knew if she was returned, the Marino family would take that as a personal slight and consider her failure as a reflection on the family, especially since she shared the last name. There was no way they would let that go unpunished. She really didn't give a fuck what happened to either Luca or Anton. Sofia was out to protect herself and if her self-preservation meant she was going to have to spend a few days with the two goons who purchased her, then so be it.

"Meaning that if we let you go, they will come find us and kill us both," Anton growled. "Just letting you go isn't an option, Sofia. If we do, we piss off the Marinos. If we take you back to the Gallo family, Isabella will have our balls and I'm rather fond of them," Anton teased. "So, for now you stay with us," he said.

"Are you going to force me to have sex with you?"

she asked. God, she hated having to ask that question but she assumed that was what she had been purchased for. "I have to warn you that I won't let that happen. I'd die first," she promised.

Luca looked her over again and she had to admit the way he looked at her made her a little uncomfortable. "We won't touch you," Luca said. "You have my promise." Sofia nodded not quite able to speak past the lump in her throat.

"Thank you," she whispered. Sofia wasn't sure if her luck had really turned but she wouldn't argue. For the first time in days she felt something akin to hope and she wasn't sure if that was a good or bad thing.

LUCA

They drove for what felt like an eternity and Luca was ready to get to the hotel and settle in for the night. Sofia must have been exhausted, but she refused to sleep watching them both with a wild look in her eyes that told him that given the chance to run—she would. He hated he couldn't convince her he wasn't going to hurt her but after what she had been through he couldn't blame her.

 When Sofia appeared on that fucking stage Luca just about lost his mind. He thought she looked familiar but the instant desire that pooled deep inside his gut was too much for him to ignore. He had only felt that way with one other person—Anton. After the auctioneer announced Sofia's name he was sure she was that same kid who used to follow him around every time she was over for a play date with his youngest sister, Mila. He was about ten years older than them and having his pesky sister's friend tagging along asking him all sorts of questions was a pain in the ass. She had turned into one of the sexiest fucking women he had ever seen, with her dark hair spilling over her shoulders and her big brown eyes. He felt an unexplainable attraction to her and before he knew it, he was raising his hand to bid on her, emptying out his fucking savings account to do so.

He knew Anton and he were under strict orders from Isabella to look but not buy but he didn't give a fuck. There was no way he'd let one of those other disgusting fuckers get their hands on Sofia. They'd ruin her and he couldn't let the sweet girl he remembered from his past be tainted in that way. He hated his and Anton's night was ruined but saving Sofia was the right thing to do. He just hoped he didn't piss Ani off or land him in too much hot water with Isabella. As his "mentor", Ani would take most of the blame for his mistake and he couldn't let that happen. They needed to get some sleep, lay low and regroup if they were going to come up with a plan.

Ani pulled into a hotel and told the two of them to stay put. Luca wouldn't leave Sofia knowing she was a flight risk, so he had no problem following Anton's orders. "You know," Luca said breaking the silence, "Anton and I will not hurt you, Sofia. We want nothing from you except for you to give us the chance to keep you safe." He looked over to her as she pretended to ignore him looking out her window into the darkness.

"You expect me to believe you purchased a virgin bride and don't intend to collect your prize?" she spat, still refusing to look at him.

He couldn't help his chuckle. He loved a woman with a little spunk and from what he remembered of Sofia, she had plenty of it. He had heard about her father's screw up with the Marino family which ended up getting him killed. Luca had a feeling the apple didn't fall far from the tree; betting Sofia had the same rebellious nature as her old man had.

"I don't see how any of this is funny, Luca," she growled. "My father is dead; my mother is being held captive back at that fucking warehouse and I was sold off to be a sex slave." Luca nodded not quite sure what to say next.

"Well, if it makes you feel any better, you aren't my sex slave," Luca teased. She shot him a murderous look and he held up his hands, as if in defense. "Too soon, sorry," he said.

"Yeah—too soon. I will never be okay with any of this. Not until everyone in my so called family pays for what they did to me and my parents," she said. Luca could see the fire in her eyes and knew she was planning to do something stupid, something that would get her killed. There was no way he could let her go off now knowing Sofia's plan.

"Listen, how about we all get a good night's sleep and then we can figure all this shit out in the morning?" he asked.

Sofia seemed to weigh his words carefully and

damn he hated she didn't trust him, but that would come in time. Luca just worried she wouldn't give him that before she took off. She finally nodded, "Fine," she spat.

"Thank you, Sofia. I promise we will find a way to help you and your family," Luca swore, just as Anton opened the door to get back into the car.

"We have a problem," Ani said. "Isabella knows and has been leaving me messages. I used cash to pay for the room, so we should be good for the night but she has a wide reach." Luca knew the Gallo family matriarch wouldn't take kindly to their disobedience and there would be hell to pay, but helping Sofia was more important than saving his own ass.

"Do you trust me?" Anton asked. His pleading look nearly did Luca in. How could Ani not know he trusted him with his life?

"Of course I do, Ani," Luca said, reaching forward to stroke his hand down Anton's face. He loved the way Ani leaned into his touch as if he craved it.

"Thank you for that, Luca," he whispered. "I have a plan but you will need to do exactly as I say, no questions asked." Luca nodded but the disgruntled noise Sofia gave told him she might not be so easily convinced to trust either of them. "It's the only way to keep both of you safe and alive, Sofia," Anton amended.

"Fine," she spat. "I'll do what you say, for now but I won't trust you—either of you." Luca saw the frustration behind Anton's smile, his mask was firmly in place. If he was being honest, Luca was more hurt than frustrated by her statement but there was nothing he could do to change Sofia's mind about them.

"That's at least a start," Luca conceded. "What's the plan?" He looked at Anton knowing his friend would have a plan forming already, he always did.

Ani's smile was easy. "Let's get into the hotel and then I'll fill you in on what I'm thinking." Luca agreed and looked around the parking lot to make sure they were truly alone. He didn't want to take any chances that they were followed. Anton got out and helped Sofia from the back seat. She was still wearing that ridiculous wedding gown they dressed her in for the auction and Luca knew getting her into the hotel without attracting suspicion would be nearly impossible. He took his jacket off and wrapped it around her. She tried to push it back off her shoulders and he held it firmly in place.

"I don't need your jacket, Luca," she insisted. "I'm not cold."

"I get that, Princess," he said. "But you will draw unwanted attention in that getup and we need to get to our room unnoticed." She slipped from the back seat holding the jacket around her shoulders, stopping to look back into the SUV where Luca still sat.

"I'll wear the jacket," she said. "But I'm not a princess. I lost that title when the fucking Marino family murdered my father and sent my mother and me to that warehouse." She turned to follow Anton into the side entrance of the hotel and damn if Luca wasn't turned on by everything about that crazy ass woman. She was a spitfire and Luca could see she gave just as good as she got. He worried they haven't yet seen her best and that thought had him both hot and scared shitless.

SOFIA

Sofia followed the guys into the hotel noting they had rented only one room and she worried they were going to go back on their promises not to touch her. She looked over to the two beds in the tiny room and wondered just where she was supposed to sleep, but anything had to be more comfortable than the bed she had spent the past few nights on in that awful warehouse.

"Sofia, you take the bed away from the window and Luca and I will bunk up in that one," Anton said, pointing to the bed closest to the window.

"You don't have to do that," she whispered. "I can just sleep on the floor, it's not a big deal."

"No," Luca insisted. "You take the bed and get some sleep. You look about ready to drop."

Sofia nodded and looked down at the gown she was wearing. She couldn't exactly wear it to bed but she really didn't have any other options. "The hotel lobby had a small gift shop and while I was checking in, I grabbed you this." Anton pulled a t-shirt that was about five sizes too big for her small frame, from his jacket and handed it to her. Sofia thought it might just be the sweetest thing anyone had done for her in a long time.

"Thank you," she whispered. "May I use the bathroom?"

"You don't have to ask our permission to do things like that, Sofia," Luca told her. "I told you in the car you are not our slave. As long as you keep your end of the bargain and don't take off, you can do as you please." Sofia nodded and turned to use the bathroom, hoping to take a quick shower. She needed to get her unruly emotions under control because she felt as though she would burst into tears at any moment and she had avoided crying all evening. She didn't want to start now.

Sofia studied her reflection in the mirror, wrapped in a fluffy white towel, fresh from the shower. She felt as though she had lived more life than her twenty-one years in just a few short days. The dark circles under her eyes were proof of the lack of sleep and stress she had to endure. She brushed her teeth with the toothbrush Anton picked up for her in the lobby and pulled the t-shirt over her head letting her wet hair fall down her back. She felt naked, vulnerable and afraid. She thought she had cried out all her tears in the shower but she was wrong, feeling the sting of fresh tears in her eyes. God, she hated crying. She was never a cry baby; never given the option. Her parents raised her to be strong and not show weakness in something as fruitless as tears. Her father used to tell her to stop her crying and go do something to change her situation if she was so unhappy. Sofia wasn't sure how to change her current problems but she was sure going to try.

She was starting to remember Luca from when she was just a kid. She had such a crush on him and would often request a playdate with Mila only to ditch her and chase Luca around. She pestered the hell out of him and was surprised he even bothered to come to her rescue tonight. She made pesky kid sister's friend seem like an understatement. He was older than she was by about ten years and when he finally left to join the Gallos she stopped asking to hang out over at Mila's. She was a shitty friend; she knew that now. Sofia had no friends left, past or present and most of that was her fault. She could only blame her father for so much of her unhappiness. The truth of it was, she created a good deal of her troubles for herself. It was time for that all to change, starting now.

She needed to convince the guys she was going to do as they asked, even go along with them for a while. Sofia was sure the Marino family wasn't going to let her stay with two of the Gallo's top men and from what she understood from their conversations in the car, Anton was Isabella's right hand guy. Once the Marinos found that out they would be out looking for her in full force. The next time they auctioned her off she might not get as lucky with who buys her. Luca and Anton had been perfect gentlemen so far and she was relieved they hadn't tried anything—yet. Sofia was taught at a young age to trust no one and apparently that included her own father. Her mother and she were paying the price for his fuck-ups and she just needed to figure out a way to break away from who she was and start a new life. But that would be easier said than done.

Sofia gingerly opened the bathroom door, peeking out, checking to see what the guys were up to. She found them sitting on the bed they were to share together and the way they were so closely talking reminded her of the two men she spied kissing the day before in front of the warehouse. It was like deja vu and she was sure they were the same guys she saw out of her window.

"You were the guys kissing on the docks outside the warehouse yesterday, weren't you?" she whispered, entering the room. Luca jumped up from the bed, releasing Anton's hand.

"What?" he questioned.

"You two were outside the warehouse yesterday afternoon, weren't you?" she asked. Anton reluctantly nodded his head and she knew she had guessed correctly.

She couldn't help her laugh, "I don't judge," she said holding her hands up. "You two can do whatever and whoever you want." Sofia giggled at her own little joke, but both guys didn't seem to find her as funny. "I'm just relieved is all," she admitted.

"Relieved?" Luca asked.

"Sure." She shrugged. "If you two are, you know—

together, than you were being honest about not touching me." Anton looked pissed and she was afraid she had overstepped. "I didn't mean to offend you in any way, Anton," she offered.

His smile replaced his anger and she could tell he was hiding part of himself away. She had known men like Anton all her life. They were good at putting their masks in place when they didn't want you to see their true selves. The question was—who Anton was and what was he hiding. He intrigued her and she almost wanted to know more about him, but that would mean she would have to stick around and actually give a damn about either of them. And, that couldn't happen.

"I think you might have misunderstood the whole situation, Princess," Anton hissed. His mask might have been in place but his words showed every ounce of his anger. "Luca and I are bi—we like men and women," he explained.

Sofia rolled her eyes at his explanation of what the word "bi" meant. Did he think she was an idiot? "I know what bi means, Anton," she sassed. "I guess I just assumed you were gay. My mistake." She tried to cover herself with her arms but there was no hiding any of her extra curves in the t-shirt she had on. It barely covered her thighs. Luca looked her body up and down and smiled.

"You saw us kissing yesterday?" Luca questioned. She nodded, not sure how to explain just how sexy it was to watch the two of them together was for her. The way Luca's big body pushed Anton up against the wall and how he took Anton's mouth in a hard passionate kiss did it for her. But, she would never admit that to either of them.

"Can we please just change the subject?" she whispered. The last thing she wanted to do was stand in a tiny hotel room with two hot as sin men talking about how hot their kiss was yesterday.

Luca laughed and Sofia felt as though he was making fun of her. She could feel a fresh wave of tears pooling in her eyes and she hated she was going to cry in front of either of them. She wiped at her cheeks as tears spilled down her face and Luca immediately sobered. He crossed the small room in just two steps and pulled her against his body. She knew it was wrong to want to be in his arms, but her traitorous body didn't even put up a fight. A sob escaped her chest as she softly cried into his shirt. Anton quickly flanked her side rubbing his hand up and down her back. It was all so sweet the way they were so freely offering her their comfort.

"I'm sorry," Luca whispered. He kissed the top of her head and for a split second, Sofia was that little girl who dreamed of just this moment with him.

"Thank you," she murmured against his chest wrapping her arms around his waist. Luca was so big and being trapped between the two of them made her feel like she was completely surrounded and safe from every outside threat, but she wasn't and she needed to remember that. Sofia reluctantly released Luca and smiled up at them both, taking a step back from them.

"I'm the one who should be sorry," she offered. "I guess the stress of the past few weeks has finally caught up to me. I can't seem to turn the water works off. I appreciate everything you both have done for me but you don't have to protect me. I can handle myself."

Anton's smile was back in place. "We get that, Princess. But, you have to understand that what we did tonight was against family orders. Once both families realize you are with us, none of us will be safe anywhere. The Marinos will be hunting you down and unless I can convince Isabella otherwise the Gallos will be coming after Luca and me. All in all—we're fucked, any way you look at it."

Sofia knew he was right. She had already figured out the part about the Marinos coming after her but she didn't know that Luca and Anton saving her ass would cost them their own lives. She couldn't let either of them go down for pulling her out of that hell hole.

"How can we stop any of that from happening?" she asked. She already knew the answer—they couldn't. He was right, they were all fucked.

"I have an idea," Anton offered. "It's probably going to piss you off Luca, but I have a few things I need to explain to you before I get to the part about my plan. I need to know you'll keep an open mind and at least hear me out. If you don't like what I have to say you walk out of here and tell everyone that bidding on Sofia was my deal. You tell Isabella you had nothing to do with anything that happened tonight and you should be fine. I'll get Sofia someplace safe and then figure out my next move."

Luca's expression was murderous and Sofia found herself taking another step back from the two of them, sure Luca was going to punch Anton in the face. "There is no fucking way I'm going to let you take the fall for any of this, Ani," he growled. "Saving Sofia was my idea and there is no way I'll leave you alone in this. I don't care what you are about to tell me, I won't leave you." Luca reached for Anton's hand and the heat between the two of them made Sofia hot. She could feel the tension, the electricity between them and she felt her own breath hitch, waiting for what she hoped would happen next. Luca pulled Anton into his big body and kissed his way into Anton's mouth. The kiss was so raw, so passionate, Sofia was sure that she had never seen anything like it, not even in the movies. A part of her wondered just what it would feel like to have someone kiss her that way.

Luca broke their kiss leaving both men panting for air. She felt out of breath herself just from watching the two of them together. "Fuck that was hot," she whispered. She didn't intend to say those words out loud.

"Yeah, it was," Luca agreed. "How about we all sit down and let Ani tell his story and then we come up with a plan to save all of our asses?" Luca looked between her and Anton and they both nodded their agreement. "Good," he said. "And can we please order some food? I'm starving." His question had both her and Anton laughing. She had to admit; she was starving too.

"I could eat," she said, shrugging.

"Fine, I'll call down to the kitchen and see if we can get some food sent up. Then we talk," Anton ordered. Sofia didn't know what Anton had to tell Luca, but from the look on his handsome face she was sure it wasn't going to be good news. She just hoped like hell she wasn't letting desire cloud her judgement. She wouldn't deny she was attracted to the two of them, but if push came to shove, she'd walk away to save her own ass. It was who she was. It was ingrained in her to be a mafia princess and she'd always look out for herself, no matter the cost.

ANTON

Anton ordered food for the three of them and had it sent to their room. He had to admit he was starving but he was too nervous to eat. What he was about to tell Luca might end not only their partnership at work, but also everything they were building together personally. He had to take the chance; otherwise, they would all be in danger and he couldn't live with himself if something happened to Luca.

"Will you please stop pacing and eat your dinner?" Luca said around a mouthful of burger. "You're making me a fucking nervous wreck." Anton sat in the room's only chair and watched as Sofia finished off her dinner. The poor woman had to be either starving or really liked what he ordered for her. Anton wondered just how long the Marino family had held her captive at the warehouse and if they bothered to feed her.

"How long were you in the warehouse?" Anton asked. He knew she might not like him prying, but he was too curious about the gorgeous brunette not to ask. She was classically beautiful, with her long dark hair and her big brown eyes. Honestly, she was just the type of woman Anton usually went after, but the scared lost look in her eyes warned him to back off.

"A few days," she admitted. "I was leaving my apartment to go to the gym and a black SUV pulled up beside me and two of the family's goons got out and pushed me into the back seat. I thought for sure they were going to kill me." Luca pushed his food back and moved to sit on the bed, next to Sofia. He wrapped an arm around her and she didn't hide the sob that bubbled up from her chest. Anton hated she had to go through all of that.

"It must have been a terrifying experience," Anton offered.

Sofia nodded leaning into Luca, accepting his comfort. "Yeah," she whispered. "The worst part was I actually wished for them to just end it all for me. It would have been easier than all of this." She motioned around her and Luca's growl filled the small hotel room.

"No fucking way," he barked. "You dying wouldn't be better than being here with us, Sofia. We want to help you, if you give us a chance." Anton nodded his head, agreeing with Luca.

"He's right, Princess," Anton said. "We really aren't worse than death." He smiled at her and she gave a half-hearted giggle.

"That's not quite what I meant. I guess I could have

ended up in a lot worse situations than I am currently in. I just don't want to live my life waiting for the other shoe to drop. Do you know what I mean?" she asked.

"I do," Anton admitted. "That's my everyday life."

"What did your father do to the Marinos?" Luca asked.

Sofia shrugged, "I have no idea," she admitted. "My father wasn't one to share. He kept my mother and I in the dark claiming if something ever went south, we'd be safe." Sofia laughed. "Best laid plans, right?"

"I have a guy who might be able to help us find out what happened to your father," Anton offered. Sofia looked at him as if he had lost his mind and maybe he had. His lead was his detective brother-in-law, Nick James, and he'd have to come clean with them both as to how he got the information on Sofia's father. Hell, if he was going to go through with sharing his plan with them he'd have to spill all the sordid details.

"Why would it matter now? The deed is done—the family has my mother and just held me captive for two days, selling me off like a piece of meat. How will knowing what my father did help me now?" she asked. Anton could feel her anger but he didn't believe she was angry with him. She was bitter about her situation and what her father had done to her and her mother.

"Right, sorry," Anton murmured.

"He was just trying to help," Luca defended. Anton smiled over at his partner and nodded. He loved how Luca always had his back, no matter what. He just hoped that held true after he spilled his guts to them.

"It's not your fault." Sofia sighed. "It's me," she offered.

"You've been through a hell of a lot these past few days. I'm sure it hasn't been easy on you since they killed your father. You have every right to be angry," Anton said.

"I'll never be safe, not once the family figures out that two guys from the Gallo's bought me." Sofia shivered.

"Well, I might have a plan that will keep all of us safe," Anton said. He knew this part might lose him his best friend and partner but he had to take a leap of faith. It might be his only option to get them all out of this mess.

"Let's have it," Luca agreed. "We are going to be in plenty of hot water ourselves with Isabella for going against orders. I'm the one who fucked up, Ani. I'll do whatever it takes to keep you and Sofia safe." Anton appreciated Luca's confidence in him. He just hoped the big guy felt the same in a few minutes.

"What I'm about to tell you Luca—well it could change everything between us," Anton whispered the last part. Luca stood and crossed the room to where Anton was sitting and pulled him up from his chair. Anton willingly let him and when Luca sealed his mouth over his; he didn't give a fuck that they had an audience. Judging from Sofia's gasp she liked watching the two of them together. Anton could feel her eyes on them watching and if he wasn't mistaken, he could hear her breathing hitch as if she was turned on by the whole scene.

"What's happening between the two of us will never change," Luca demanded, breaking their kiss. Anton had to admit he found the whole thing hot and the way Luca looked at him had him feeling as if he might burst into flames.

"Thank you for that, Luca," Anton said linking their fingers together. He needed the connection to Luca. "I've been working both sides of the fence," he murmured.

Luca's whole body went rigid and Anton knew he hit a nerve. "Wanna say that again, Ani?" Luca asked.

"I've been turning over evidence to bring down major crime families in Chicago and New York. One of my brothers-in-law is a New York City police detective. He worked undercover in the Gallo organization for a while until he was made. I've been feeding him evidence for over a year now," Anton said. Luca dropped his hand and Anton instantly regretted his honesty. Luca paced the floor which was no easy feat with how big he was. He took up half the room and Anton finally stood in his path, not able to take any more.

"Please just let me finish," Anton begged. Luca shot him an incredulous look and Anton knew he was on a very short leash.

"You have my attention," Luca spat.

"Thank you, Luca," Anton whispered. "Please believe I didn't make this decision easily. Last year,

Isabella forced me into the family and I've been looking for a way out ever since. She was going after my family—my mother and my sister Valentine. I couldn't stand by and let Isabella hurt them so I made a deal with her. I would help her bring down the Marino family if she let my family walk."

"The Gallos have been trying to bring down the Marinos since before any of us were born," Sofia said. She stood between the two of them and Anton wasn't sure if he was making a mistake by involving her. He needed to remember Sofia's last name was Marino and he didn't know her. She could very well turn around and use everything he was telling her against him and Luca. Where would they be then?

"I know that," Anton said. "I used what I had to save my family. I was lucky enough to be given a list of names of Marino family members who were working with the Feds. I showed Isabella my proof and she, in turn, let my family walk away—no strings attached."

"Fuck," Luca swore. "What the hell were you thinking, Ani? No one walks away from the family."

"Isabella likes me. She told me I remind her of her husband when she first met him," Anton admitted. Luca made a face and Anton chuckled. "It's not like that man. She treats me like one of her sons. Hell, she treats me better than any of her sons." Anton shrugged. "Maybe I just got lucky, I don't know. But after I made the deal, my sister has been allowed to live her life back in New York with her two husbands and my mother."

"Two husbands?" Sofia questioned. She looked

between Luca and Anton and her cheeks turned the cutest shade of pink. Anton smiled at her and nodded.

"Two," he confirmed.

"So, what happened once you turned the evidence over to Isabella?" Luca questioned. He seemed determined to get to the rest of Anton's story.

"Nothing at first. But then I noticed some of the smaller cells in the Marino family began to dissipate. I gave the same list to my brother-in-law and his department worked with the Feds to bring in the members of the family who had turned. Most of them made it out of the Marino organization and Isabella was none the wiser. She counted their disappearances as a win, believing the intel she fed to her contacts in the Marino family led to the men being discovered and murdered as traitors. Her goal was to let the family tear itself apart and when she realized that was slowly happening over time, she believed it was all her own doing. Isabella never questioned me having her back and I've worked hard to keep it that way—until now."

"What changed?" Luca asked. "Why are you telling me this now?"

"Because I think Nick can help us," he offered. "If we go back to Isabella with Sofia she'll see what we did as an act of betrayal. If we don't go back to her the Marinos will catch up with us and take Sofia and probably kill us, just for sport. Either way we're fucked. If we can get to New York I know that Nick will help us. We can make a fresh start," Anton offered.

Luca seemed like he wanted to pace the floor again

but Sofia and Anton flanked his sides. He looked like a caged animal, ready to break out. "Maybe I misjudged the situation, Luca. I'm sorry. I thought we might be past the point of keeping secrets from each other," Anton whispered. "Like I said earlier. If you don't like my plan, I'll go back to Isabella and tell her this was all my fault. You and Sofia should be safe that way," he offered.

"No," Luca barked. Anton wanted to argue with him, but from the look on Luca's handsome face he wouldn't have it. "I'm in, Ani. Where you go, I go and to hell with the family," he growled.

They both looked at Sofia, as if expecting her to make some grand gesture to join their secret club and judging from her smile, she was on board. "Well, I've always wanted to go to New York," she sassed. Anton wasn't sure how he was going to pull this off, but if he could get them all safely to his sister's place in New York, he'd be able to keep Luca and Sofia safe. There was really no other option.

LUCA

"So, what do we do next?" Luca asked. Anton had always been a little mysterious and Luca guessed it was one of the things that had drawn him in. He always liked his men to be edgy and Ani didn't disappoint. He thought it was because his partner had so much responsibility on his shoulders. Luca knew it must have been a hell of a lot of pressure being Isabella's right hand man. The way the old broad seemed to dote on Ani always made him wonder just what was going on between the two of them, but hearing how she treated him as one of her sons helped him to breathe a little easier.

"Now, I call Nick and have him try to get us out of here," Anton said. "He has people who he trusts in the area. His team has been working to extract the members of the Marino family who turned before the family could find out who they were and take matters into their own hands." Anton looked at Sofia and didn't seem to miss the same undertone of sadness in her Luca saw. Her father wasn't so lucky. He didn't escape the family and Sofia and her mom were paying the price. Luca hated she had been through hell but he was hoping she'd let them help her. If he was being completely honest, he wanted to do a whole lot more than just help Sofia Marino. She was his walking wet dream and seeing her in nothing but a t-shirt with her wet hair spilling down her back in curls, made him half-crazy with lust. Being in the same room with both Sofia and Ani had his body revved up ready to play, but he knew now wasn't the time.

He didn't know much about Anton's family. Being born into a mob family you learn quickly not to ask too many questions or get involved in anyone else's business. He and Ani knew what it was like to lose family because someone asked too many questions. Luca had heard about Anton's dad and how he was offed by the Gallos. Families didn't care if you had blood ties to an organization or not. Disloyalty was not allowed and if you were caught, you weren't given a second chance. Luca knew that all too well. He had messed up and went against Isabella's orders now a few times. Each time he waited for the hammer to drop but he merely got a slap on the wrists. A part of him wondered if Anton had something to do with her leniency but he never asked.

Luca had trouble seeing past the whole right versus wrong issues most of the family members had no problem overlooking. They were like trained monkeys out to do Isabella's bidding at any cost—even their own souls. He couldn't be that man. Luca oversaw shaking down business owners for their "rents", as Isabella like to call it. Really, it was hush money or he'd even call it protection money, although he was sure the businesses were paying for protection from the Gallo family. When they refused to pay, his team had to be persuasive and sometimes that got ugly. He usually tried to keep his hands clean, turning a blind eye to the men who he sent in to do the persuading. But, the last couple times he just didn't have it in him to flex his muscles. He went back to Isabella trying to plead the business owner's case for an extension and she outright refused, telling him he had gone soft. Maybe she was right, maybe he had but there was no way he could go against what he believed in, even if it meant saving his own ass.

Luca had always lived on the edge of good and evil and those blurred lines were what usually landed him in hot water. His father was Anthony Sr.'s brother, which meant Luca had no choice but to join the family once he was of age. Having the last name of Gallo didn't afford him many options. He knew the score; he was groomed from a young age to know his place in the family's business. He took up where his father left off, collecting the rents. His dad had dementia and eventually couldn't perform his duties. He and Luca's mom were now living in Florida but they came back to Chicago to visit. He loved how he could take his father's place; it was tradition and gave his dad the peace of mind he needed to leave the city and enjoy the time he had left.

"You two wait here," Anton ordered. "I'm going to call Nick and set things up." Luca nodded and pulled Sofia into his body, watching Anton leave the small hotel room. He was surprised she let him but after their crazy night together, nothing should shock him.

"Do you believe him?" Sofia looked up at him and his damn heart felt as though it was beating out of his chest.

"I do. I trust Ani with my life," Luca whispered. "I knew Anton had pull with the family, I just never imagined he also had a police detective in his pocket. The question is, do you believe him, Sofia?" He almost didn't want to know her answer. He could still see her wheels turning as if she was trying to figure out her next move. Luca worried she might still decide to run even though she promised not to. The thought of Sofia being out in the world alone and possibly in trouble again did strange things to his heart.

"I'm not sure," she answered, "about any of this."

"Even me?" Luca questioned. He knew her when she was just a kid but would it be enough to earn her trust now? Luca turned her in his arms not letting her hide from him and when she looked into his eyes, he could see his answer. She trusted him, even if she didn't want to.

"I can't explain why I feel this way but I do trust you, Luca. You probably remember me as a pesky brat who followed you around like a complete nuisance.

God, I was awful to your poor sister. Mila just wanted to hang out and play barbies and all I could think about was how cute her brother was." Sofia giggled and shook her head. "After you left home, I stopped asking Mila for play dates. I'm pretty sure she caught on I wasn't there to see her. I was a complete ass to her."

Luca laughed at the memory. "You were pretty annoying at the time. Mila gave as good as she got though. Out of all my sisters she's the worst." Luca used to hate being the only boy. As the oldest it was his responsibility to watch out for his sisters and he couldn't beat the guys up fast enough, to keep them away from his siblings. Mila was the only one left not married. She decided to go to college and get her degree in fashion rather than settle down and have a big Italian family. She hated tradition and ran as far away from home as soon as she turned eighteen.

"She's living in California now and going to college out there," he said. "Do you still think Mila's brother is cute?" he asked. Luca wanted to kick himself for just blurting the question out. He shouldn't care what Sofia thought of him, but he did. She looked up at him through her long lashes and hesitantly licked her lips. He couldn't help the small moan that escaped his chest. Everything about sexy little Sofia turned him on. Having his arms around her and her body pressed up against his was almost too much for his overactive libido to take.

She shyly nodded and smiled up at him. Luca couldn't help himself, he pulled her up his body and kissed his way into her mouth. He tried to remind himself to be gentle with her, she had been through so much in the past couple of days, but he couldn't help himself. He felt like he wanted to consume her and his raw need for her took over. He kissed and nipped his way into her mouth and when she wrapped her arms around his neck, he completely lost control of his senses, pushing her down onto the bed and covering her sexy curves with his own body. He needed her more than he needed air and from the way Sofia responded to him, she felt the same way.

"Tell me to stop, Sofia," Luca begged, as he kissed his way down her neck.

"Why would I do that?" she whispered. Sofia ran her fingers through his hair giving the ends a little tug. He liked how rough she was with him. "I want you, Luca. I have since we were kids but I'm not a little girl anymore. I want you to take my virginity, please," she begged.

Luca rolled off her body and laid next to her on the bed panting as if he had just run a race. "Fuck," he spat.

"Why did you stop, Luca?" she asked. He could hear the hurt in her voice and that was the last thing he wanted. But taking her virginity wasn't the right thing to do. She should be offering it to someone else, someone worthy of such a gift. He wasn't that man.

"I'm not right for you, Sofia. I want things you can't give me and making you mine—taking your virginity would be wrong." He watched as Sofia stood up from the bed readjusting her t-shirt.

"Fine," she spat. "I'll just ask Anton to do it then." He almost wanted to laugh at the way she looked at him. He was reminded of the bratty little girl who followed him around, all those years ago.

"Ask Anton what?" Ani asked, walking into the room. He looked between Sofia and Luca and waited for one of them to clue him in.

"She wants for you to take her virginity since I just refused," Luca said. Anton looked Luca up and down as if he could see right through him. Luca was sure his friend would be able to tell he wanted Sofia just from the erection he sported from having her pressed up against his body.

"You won't take her virginity?" Anton questioned.

"No," Sofia whispered. "He doesn't want me," she said with a pout.

"Oh Princess, he wants you all right," Anton scoffed. "Look at his fucking cock. If he wanted you any more he'd burst through the zipper of his pants." Luca looked down at his unruly dick and back up to Anton with a triumphant smile plastered across his face. He loved the way Ani knew him.

Sofia gasped when she turned to see just what Anton was talking about. She couldn't seem to stop looking at him and Luca could feel her hot stare as if it scorched him. "Fuck, Sofia," he growled. "Stop looking at me that way," he ordered. She bit her bottom lip into her mouth and Luca couldn't help his frustrated growl. If she didn't stop looking at him like she wanted to make a meal out of him he was going to burst in his pants. He grabbed a pillow from the bed and covered his cock, blocking Sofia's prying gaze. She giggled and turned back to face Anton.

"So, how about it, Anton?" she asked. Luca was starting to wonder where the shy, scared woman went from earlier. Everything about Sofia was bold and daring and he was sure she was going to be his and Anton's undoing.

Luca stared down Anton as if trying to warn him to turn their mafia princess down, but from the look on Ani's face, turning Sofia down was the last thing he wanted to do. Anton crossed the room and sat down on the bed pulling Sofia to sit on his lap. Luca wanted to tell him to get his fucking hands off her, but seeing them together made him hot. He was never one to sit on the sidelines and he wasn't going to start now. Luca sat down beside them and pulled Sofia's legs across his lap. It felt oddly right for the three of them to be sitting there that way, but Luca wouldn't allow himself to get his hopes up for something that would probably never happen.

"Why do you want to have sex so badly, Sofia?" Anton asked. Luca almost wanted to laugh at his question but honestly, he wanted to know the same thing.

"I hear all the kids are doing it so I thought I'd give it a shot," she sassed. Luca laughed and Anton shot him a heated glare.

"This is serious, Sofia. If you want us to jump into bed with you then you need to tell us why," Anton said.

Sofia looked between the two of them and didn't say anything. Finally she sighed and leaned into Ani's body.

"If something goes wrong with your plan and the Marinos get their hands on me again and I'm still a virgin, this nightmare will just start all over. Virgins sell for a whole lot more than women who have been used," she whispered. Luca hated hearing the fear in Sofia's voice. He wished she knew he and Ani had her back and would do everything in their power to keep her safe.

Anton wrapped his arms around her and Luca was sure he was going to give into Sofia's request. "I'm sorry, Sofia. I won't take your virginity just for the sake of doing so. You're safe with us Princess. Luca and I won't let anyone hurt you again. And when we do take your virginity it won't be because you are afraid but because you are desperate with need for both of us."

Sofia sat up and looked between the two of them, "Both?" she asked. Luca liked the way her breath hitched when Anton nodded his answer. He had to admit, hearing how Ani wanted them both to take her made him crazy with need. Luca wanted them both and hopefully Sofia and Anton would be his soon because he wasn't a patient man.

SOFIA

Sofia wasn't sure what to say to Anton admitting they both wanted her. She could see the evidence of Luca wanting her. She felt it in the way he kissed her, as if she was his last meal. Honestly, she felt the same way about him but he was too damn honorable to do anything about her situation. That was the way she thought about her virginity, as a situation that needed to be dealt with. The sooner she took care of her little problem, the sooner she could move on with her life and stop worrying the Marinos would catch up with her again. Maybe if she was worth less to them they would let her walk away. And if she was being completely honest, she wanted them both too, but the idea of them taking her together both terrified her and turned her on.

"We both want you, Sofia," Luca confirmed. "But you have to understand what that means. Anton and I are just trying to figure this all out as we go. We've never done anything about our own feelings and tossing you into the mix might be too much for you. If you want to be with us—both of us—then it means you accept Ani and I together. We won't hide who we are anymore. I've been running and hiding my whole life and I'm fucking done with that. If we are going to make a fresh start then the three of us will need to come up with some ground rules."

"Like?" she asked. Sofia couldn't believe she was even considering the whole threesome thing. She hadn't even had a twosome, but she knew she didn't want to hide from her feelings. She wanted both Anton and Luca. Watching them together, every time they kissed, was hot as hell.

"Like—no jealousy. We are together because we want to be and jealousy will have no place in whatever we build," Anton said.

"Agreed," Luca said. "We make decisions together when they concern the three of us. We won't take over your life but we won't let you hurt us, Sofia. If you decide to walk away that's on you, but you have to know your actions will affect both Ani and me."

"I have to admit, before you found me I was planning on running. Hell, I was planning on taking my own life rather than letting someone have my body. I had it all worked out in my mind, but then the two of you bid on me and now—you're giving me a chance. I won't run," she promised. Luca's sexy smile made her melt and Sofia knew she made the right decision.

"Thank you, Sofia," Luca said. "I know it isn't easy

for you to trust anyone right now. You've been through so much already. I promise not to let you down."

"So, does that mean you will take my virginity?" she hopefully asked. Luca looked at Anton and back at her. She could tell he wanted to say yes to her but Luca was letting him call the shots. Anton shook his head.

"No," Luca grumbled. "Although I have to say I'm not on board with that decision, Ani," he said.

"Me either." Sofia looked back over her shoulder at Anton and he shrugged.

"We need to get a good night's sleep and figure the rest of our shit out. Getting naked and sweaty sounds good but we can't let our guard down. Isabella tried to call me while I was on the phone with Nick. She's not going to just give up on trying to find us. We can't take any chances," Anton said.

"What did your brother-in-law say?" Sofia questioned. She felt as though she was prying but she really couldn't help it. Her choices were taken away from her and she just wanted to be back in the loop. Sofia needed to feel as though she was a contributing member of their little group or this threesome wasn't going to work for her. She was done letting everyone else make decisions for her. First, her father and then the Marino family. That wasn't her life now and if she was going to make a fresh start for herself and possibly move forward with Anton and Luca, she would have her say.

"He is buying the airline tickets and will email me the information. I have a secure account we use to talk;

one that isn't tied to the family. Nick will send me over the tickets and has even planned on having one of his contacts meet us to give me some new IDs for the three of us. We have to become someone else for this to work." Anton put Sofia onto the bed and she cuddled into Luca's body wanting the comfort. Anton stood from the bed and started to strip out of his suit, down to just his boxers. She could feel Luca's breath hitch and Sofia had to admit; she felt the exact same way. Anton was hot underneath his business attire with his chiseled abs and muscles. He definitely worked out and the sight of him had her itching to touch him all over.

"I figured Sofia doesn't have any identification on her and you and I need to lay low," Anton offered. Sofia wanted to giggle at the way Luca was watching him. She was sure he didn't hear a word Anton just said.

"For now, I say we get some shuteye and tomorrow morning I'll run out to get us some new clothes. We can't have Sofia running around the city in a wedding dress. That will draw some undue attention and that's the last thing we want," Anton said. He yawned and stretched and she let her gaze follow his body. Luca seemed about ready to crawl out of his own skin.

"Fuck, Ani," Luca exclaimed. "How am I supposed to sleep next to you when you do shit like that?" he growled. Anton shot them both a sexy smirk and Sofia wondered if he knew exactly what he was doing to them both.

"Well, I was thinking about that," Anton said. "It's a king size bed so why don't the three of us share?"

Sofia wanted to tell him no. She had never slept with a man in her life and the thought of being wedged between the two of them all night long, made her uneasy. If she was going to agree to their offer of a threesome she would need to get used to being caught up between their two big bodies. It was time to put up or shut up, as her father used to say. She wanted to agree and there was no way she'd back down from them now.

"Fine by me," she said, trying for casual but sure she failed.

Luca chuckled and stood from the bed stripping out of his clothes down to his boxer briefs. God, his body was even better than she ever imagined. When she was a kid she'd catch glimpses of Luca without his shirt. He would be outside his house washing his car and she wouldn't be able to stop herself from staring out of Mila's window. But now, Luca had filled out to be more than she ever imagined. His body was bigger than Anton's, but not by much. He had a sleeve of tattoos over one of his pecks and down his shoulder covering his entire arm. She wondered if he'd let her get a good look at his tats. Hell, she hoped he'd let her trace his tats with her tongue but she'd save that question for another time. Anton's heated gaze roamed over Luca's body and Sofia could tell he was just as turned on by the hulk of a man. Luca flashed them both a wolfish grin and she could tell he was liking all the attention they were giving him.

Luca climbed into bed and reached for Sofia,

pulling her into the middle of the mattress. Anton took his place on the other side of her and she felt warm and protected—safe for the first time in weeks. The thought crossed her mind that she could get used to being between them and she worried she was getting ahead of herself. They didn't promise her forever—hell, they didn't even promise her long term. Sofia needed to remember she would have to keep her feelings and emotions in check. This whole world might be new to her, but it wasn't for the guys and she knew letting her heart get tangled up between them was a dangerous game—one she couldn't afford to play and lose.

ANTON

Anton woke the next day tangled up in a mesh of arms and legs. Luca and Sofia were both cuddlers and trying to slip from the bed proved almost impossible. When he was finally free he pulled his cell from his jacket pocket and found a bunch of missed phone calls from Isabella and the promised e-mail from Nick. He knew if they were going to make their plane he would have to run out to find them some clothes. He slipped into his suit and left a note for Luca on the night table. He hated leaving the two of them. They seemed so content, but he knew their reprieve would be short lived. Knowing Isabella like he did, he knew she would have an army of men out looking for them. He also knew he wouldn't be able to avoid Isabella's phone calls for much longer and he knew just what he had to do to head her off. He would just have to feed her enough lies to throw her off their trail, at least until they were all safely in New York. But, that would also involve a face to face meeting with his boss that he might not walk away from.

He chanced one last look back into the dark room where Luca and Sofia were still sleeping, snuggled together and whispered a little prayer he'd see them again. Anton knew if he woke Luca to tell him where he was going he would insist on going with him. He knew Luca tagging along to his meeting with Isabella wouldn't end well for him.

On the way to his car Anton sent Isabella a text politely asking her to meet with him at her favorite restaurant, Maria's Italian Kitchen. It was owned by Anton's great-grandmother, Maria. Isabella and his mother used to work there when they were teenagers. He was hoping reminding Isabella they were family would earn him some trust, but he knew all too well having family in common didn't always warrant leniency. The last time he was at Maria's was when he had to say goodbye to his mother and sister after he convinced Isabella to let them walk away from the family. He had very limited contact with his mother and Valentine now. He usually got his updates from one of his sister's husbands. Anton didn't want to involve his sister or mother in family business again. He hoped someday they would all be together when he was free and clear of the Gallo family but he also knew that dream might never come true for him.

Isabella texted back quickly letting him know she would be there and he breathed a sigh of relief. He needed to grab a few things for their trip to New York and then he'd meet with Isabella and lie his ass off. Their lives depended on her believing him and Anton just hoped his charm won the way out of his current mess with his boss. He shot Luca a message, letting him know he had a few errands to run and if he wasn't back in time, to get on the plane to New York. He forwarded their flight information Nick had sent him, not wanting to take any chances with Sofia or Luca's safety.

A few minutes after he hit send, Luca called him. He thought about not answering, but then he knew Luca well enough to know he wouldn't allow Anton to ignore him. Luca would go off and do something stupid, getting them all killed and that was exactly what Anton was trying to avoid.

"What the fuck is going on, Ani?" Luca barked into the phone. Anton smiled at his tone. Luca seemed to only have one volume but when he was pissed, he didn't hold back, not even with Anton.

"I'm getting us all some clothes for our trip and had a few lose ends to tie up," Anton said. It wasn't really a lie; he just omitted the part where he was going to meet with Isabella.

"You're going to do something stupid aren't you, Ani? Is that why you told us to get on the plane if you're not back in time?" Luca always seemed to be able to read him and that fact shouldn't surprise Anton as much as it did.

"I told you I have a few loose ends to tie up, Luca," Anton said. "You just keep Sofia safe and when I get back we can talk about this. Right now I need to go."

Anton pulled up to the restaurant and noticed how heavily guarded the place was. Isabella wasn't taking any chances with him and he couldn't fault her. He fucked up and she would want her pound of flesh.

He disconnected the call to a string of curses coming from the other end of the line and didn't hide his amusement. Luca's creative use of the English language always made him laugh. He took a deep breath and let it out. "It's now or never," he mumbled to himself, stepping from the SUV.

Anton nodded to the guards posted at the front entrance of the restaurant. He knew them both personally and he didn't miss their looks of pity. They probably considered him a dead man walking but they didn't know he had an ace up his sleeve. He had a plan and if Isabella bought his story he'd be walking back out of there and getting on that fucking plane with Luca and Sofia.

He strolled through to where he knew Isabella would be sitting in her favorite booth in the main dining room. That's just where he found her, in the oversized red leather clad seat with a portrait of her grandmother, Maria, looking over her. The picture of his great-grandmother always made him smile. His sister Valentine looked just like Maria and his heart ached just thinking about all the time he was missing with his sister and her new family—time he'd never be able to get back.

He stood at the end of the table waiting for Isabella to issue him an invitation to sit and join her. The older woman took her good sweet time before looking up at him and offering him a seat. She plastered on her best smile but Anton could tell it wasn't genuine. Isabella was pissed and he worried no amount of groveling or lies was going to fix what he and Luca had done.

"Isabella," he nodded, "Thank you for agreeing to see me."

"You really left me no choice, Anton. I've been calling your cell phone for the past twenty-four hours since I received news you and Luca disobeyed my direct orders." Anton winced at Isabella's tone.

"Yes, I'm sorry about that," he lied. "We had the Marino family tailing us and we had to find a safe place to land."

Isabella shot him an incredulous look. "Why would the Marino family be after you? Didn't you buy the princess fair and square?" she asked. Anton knew Isabella would have had spies with eyes and ears everywhere. She would know the full story and he needed to be careful with how he spun the truth.

"Yes but once they figured out Luca and I were there under your orders, they sent some goons after us. I'm guessing they're worried about what information Sofia Marino will feed to the Gallo organization," he said. He noticed the flare of understanding in Isabella's eyes and she smiled at him again, this time he could tell it was genuine.

"So, you disobeyed orders to nab a mafia princess to gather intel for me?" Isabella asked. Anton nodded hoping his boss bought the story. There was no way he could tell her Luca bid on Sofia out of sheer desire that had been building since they were kids. And he sure as hell wouldn't be giving his boss the news he and Luca had plans to put her between the two of them to make her theirs. The less Isabella knew about his and Luca's relationship, the better. Anton had always preferred to keep his private life private from Isabella.

She threw back her head and laughed, "And here I thought you two morons were thinking with your dicks."

Anton shot her his best grin. "Well, not this time. We haven't touched the princess. She's quite a handful, but she has nothing left but hatred towards the Marino family for what they did to her. She's willing to give us any information she has to help bring them down."

"I'm so happy to hear this news, Ani," Isabella admitted. "Here I thought I was going to have to mess up my cousin's restaurant with your blood. I'm sure she will be happy to hear that won't be necessary." Anton grimaced at the thought of literally having just dodged a bullet, causing Isabella to chuckle.

"When will I be able to meet Miss Marino?" Isabella asked. "I'd like to speak with her personally."

"She is very shy and has agreed to speak with Luca and me, but we don't want to spook her. She's already provided us with valuable information and we're afraid if we attempt to bring her in, she will clam up," Anton lied. He waited Isabella out and she made no signs of accepting the fact he didn't want to do as ordered and bring Sofia in for questioning. He decided Isabella might need a gentle nudge. "Plus, if we bring her to you we stand the chance of the Marino's finding us and we can't afford to lose her. Not until we get all the Intel we need from her, then we can do whatever you wish with the princess."

Isabella slowly nodded seeming to accept his explanation. "Fine, but when you have what you need from her I want her brought to me. We can't allow her to live—you do know that Ani, right?"

Anton shrugged and nodded as if he didn't give a fuck as to what happened to pretty Sofia, but there would be no way he'd ever turn her over to Isabella. No one would lay a finger on her except him and Luca. "I get it," he lied. "She's a liability and the family can't have any of those. I will personally see to this, Isabella," he promised. "We will get the information you need and bring her to you."

Isabella smiled and nodded, "Thank you, Ani. I'm sure I don't have to remind you Luca is on very thin ice with this organization. I hope he isn't becoming a bad influence on you. You've never gone against orders before and I'm wondering why now?"

"I told you I have a plan, Isabella. This was all just a part of it. I saw a gift horse and I bought her. Sofia Marino is our ticket to bringing down the whole Marino family just give Luca and me time to get the information from her. I promise we won't let you down." Anton hoped his poker face was firmly in place. He didn't want to give Isabella any hint he was lying to her. His sister used to jokingly tell him he was the worst liar she had ever met. He just hoped Isabella couldn't read him as well as Valentine could.

Isabella stood from the booth to leave. On her way out of the room she turned back to look at him. "You have your time, Anton. But, don't take too long. Keep in touch and if you make me chase you down again our next meeting won't end so well for you," she spat. He could tell from the fire he saw behind her eyes that Isabella meant every single word. She was letting him off with a stern warning this time. His next encounter with the head of the Gallo family might not end so well for him. Anton just hoped like hell there wasn't a next time. He was counting on his brother-in-law to help get the three of them out of this jam. Otherwise, he wasn't sure he'd be able to smooth things over with Isabella a second time.

LUCA

Luca paced the airport terminal not liking the fact they stood out like a sore thumb. Sofia had to wear her stupid white gown the Marinos dressed her in for the auction and she looked like a blushing bride as they sat and waited for their plane to call for passengers to board. He was using the story they were just married and headed off to New York for their honeymoon.

His biggest worry was where the hell Anton was. He hated how Ani just up and left them and the fact he probably headed straight for Isabella trying to save the two of them. He had no idea if Ani was alive or dead at this point. If Isabella was mad enough she would have refused any story Anton tried to feed her and had him dealt with. Luca wasn't sure what the hell he was supposed to do once he and Sofia got to New York, but telling Anton's family he was murdered by the Gallos wasn't the first impression he wanted to make with them.

"Do you think he'll make it in time?" Sofia whispered. She sat so close to Luca, as if needing his comfort. He linked their fingers together and gave her his best smile.

"Ani will be here," Luca promised. He just hoped like hell Anton didn't make a liar out of him. He wasn't sure how they were going to do any of this without him. Anton had become more than his business partner. They had become friends and if things had a chance to play out, Luca wanted to be so much more than that with Ani. Luca wanted him and Sofia; having one without the other wouldn't feel right to him. He knew that made him sound greedy but he didn't care. Luca finally knew what he wanted and he was going to go after them both.

The woman at the gate called for them to board and Luca waited until the last possible moment to get on the plane. He was hoping Anton would make it, but Luca knew they wouldn't hold the plane for any reason. He and Sofia boarded and stowed their sparse belongings in the overhead bins. Luca tried to remain calm and even in control but he felt anything but those things. He knew his internal panic would only upset Sofia and he wanted to be the person she could lean on. Luca would have to wait until later to fall apart when they were safely in New York.

Just as the stewardess was about to shut and secure the door Anton came running onto the plane shouting for her to hold the door. Sofia's smile nearly lit up the entire cabin and Luca felt the exact same way.

Anton thanked the stewardess for waiting for him and slipped down the aisle to where Luca and Sofia stood waiting for him. "It's about fucking time," Luca whispered. "We thought you weren't going to make it, Ani." Anton pulled him in for a hug and then turned to Sofia to do the same.

"Sorry guys. It's a long story but I'm here now," Anton said.

"You went off and did something stupid, didn't you?" Luca asked.

"Please take your seats," the stewardess said over the plane's intercom. "We are getting ready for takeoff."

They took their seats putting Sofia in the middle of them and buckled in. "I'll tell you both all about it as soon as we take off," Anton promised. Luca knew he wasn't going to like any part of Ani's story. In fact, he was sure it was going to involve Anton meeting with Isabella and that was going to piss him off.

"The most important thing is you made it and we are getting out of here in one piece," Sofia offered, taking each of their hands into her own. Luca liked the way she seemed to so willingly fit between the two of them. He was looking forward to getting to the part where they made her theirs completely. He knew they had other things to worry about, but his brain had been firing on all cylinders since finding Sofia at the auction. All he wanted to do was lay claim to both her and Ani, wanting them both to be his.

THE TRIP to New York took no time at all. They had spent most of it discussing Anton's decision to go off on his own and meet with Isabella. Luca hated how Ani didn't tell him about his plans and he worried Anton would never consider him an equal partner. If he had, Ani would have woken him to run everything by him that morning. Instead he went off on his own and didn't even consider how that would make Luca or Sofia worry. Luca kept it together on the plane not wanting to make a scene. As soon as they were all safely in the car that Anton's brother-in-law had waiting for them, he couldn't hold back his temper any longer.

"You should have fucking told us what you were planning," Luca growled. He sat in the passenger seat, letting Anton drive since he knew the area. Sofia sat in the back seat quietly watching the two of them. He could tell she had been holding back too, but she still wasn't comfortable enough to tell them how she was feeling.

Anton sighed, "I know that, Luca. I thought I was doing the right thing for all of us. If you had gone with me that would have left Sofia vulnerable. Plus, it might have put you in danger. Isabella isn't your biggest fan. What if she would have used you as an example to punish me? I would have never forgiven myself if I involved you and you took the fall for what the two of us did. I made the choice to protect you—both of you," he said, looking into the rearview mirror at Sofia.

"I appreciate that, Anton," Sofia almost whispered. "But we are a team now, aren't we?" Luca looked over to where Anton white knuckled the steering wheel waiting for him to answer. If Anton had changed his mind about the three of them he wasn't sure what he would do.

"Yeah, we're a team now," Anton finally agreed.

"Good," Luca said. "From now on none of us does anything without talking it through with the other two. Agreed?"

"Agreed," Ani and Sofia said in unison. He chuckled at how they already seemed to be in sync with each other.

"So, if we aren't really going to turn me over to the Gallo family, what's the actual plan here?" Sofia asked.

"I have no fucking idea," Anton admitted. "When I went to her this morning I wasn't quite sure how I was going to spin the whole, 'we disobeyed your orders and bought a woman', deal. Honestly, I didn't know if I was going to be walking out of that restaurant or not. All I could think about was trying to come up with a story Isabella would buy. She helped to fill in some of the blanks and I just led her to assume she had guessed correctly. Hell, she concocted half the story herself. I didn't have to do much to convince her," Ani admitted.

Luca barked out his laugh," Of course you didn't, man. That old broad loves you. You just smiled and winked at her and she bought whatever shit you were shoveling." Anton didn't seem as amused by Luca's assessment as he and Sofia were. Ani didn't seem to know just how powerful his charisma was, especially to women. They always seemed to love Ani's boyish charm and sexy as sin confidence. Plus, he was good looking and his body looked as though he spent hours in the gym every day. As Ani's workout partner, Luca knew that was basically true. The guy was like a machine with the way he pushed not only himself but Luca every morning before the sun came up.

"Well, I can't count on my charm and good looks to get me out of every situation now, can I?" Anton teased. "I say we get to my sister's house and meet with Nick. He's waiting for us there and we can all sit down and come up with a good plan." Luca liked to think Anton meant it. He wanted them to plan out their next move together as a team but he also knew Ani was used to going it alone. He would have a tough time listening to anyone else's advice.

Meeting Anton's family both thrilled and scared the shit out of him. He wondered just what Ani's family would think about the three of them together. Anton's sister was married to two guys, but he was pretty sure their relationship didn't cross the line past the two of them sharing the same woman. Luca wondered if Ani's family would accept the fact he is bi.

"Does your family know you are bringing us?" Luca asked.

"Of course," Anton said. "Nick knows what happened and that I wouldn't leave you two behind. We are in this together, remember?"

"Sure," Luca said. "I guess I'm wondering if your family knows you like men?" He could tell by the expression on Anton's face he had never broached the subject with his family. Luca hated how he pried but he had to know. He wouldn't want to out Anton to his family by being overly affectionate with him in front of them.

"No," Ani whispered. "My family doesn't know I'm bi. But, they are about to find out because I won't fucking hide you away from them, Luca. I won't hide the fact the three of us are together now."

"But we're not," Sofia said. "You know—in that way." Luca turned to see the embarrassment on her beautiful face and he wished he could touch her; tell her she was wrong.

"Just because we haven't had sex yet doesn't mean we aren't together, Princess," Anton insisted.

"Um, will we be—you know—having sex then?" She shyly asked.

"Fuck yeah we will," Luca confirmed. Anton smirked and Luca could almost read every dirty thought that ran through his mind.

"Tonight, Princess," Anton promised. Sofia's face lit up and Luca had to admit he felt the same damn way about Anton's promise. He was looking forward to making them both his.

"It will be our first time together, Ani," Luca whispered.

"It will be my first time ever," Sofia nervously admitted.

"We'll go nice and slow, baby," Luca promised. "We'll follow your lead." Sofia nodded and looked out her window at the passing city streets. Luca could tell she was nervous but he was being honest with her. He'd do whatever it took to make her comfortable. He wanted Sofia and Anton too much not to agree to just about anything they wanted.

"Nick has a place for us to stay. It's one of the safe houses he uses to help the guys who turn on their families," Anton said. "I guess we fit that mold now." Luca could hear the sadness and worry in Anton's voice and he wondered if they had made the right decision.

"I'm so sorry, guys. I feel like this is all my fault," Sofia sobbed from the back seat. There was no fucking way he'd let her take the blame for what they were about to do. Luca had wanted out of that life for a long time but he was just too afraid to admit it.

"This isn't on you, Princess," Anton growled. "I've been planning this for over a year now. I just didn't count on dragging you two into this shit storm with me."

"Well, like it or not we're in this with you now, Ani," Luca admitted and he wouldn't have it any other way. For better or worse he was Anton's partner in every sense of the word. The sooner he could tie both Sofia and Ani to him the better Luca would feel. He just had to get through the next few hours and then he would show them both how much he wanted them. There would be no turning back for any of them after tonight.

SOFIA

Sofia felt unusually shy as Anton introduced her to his family. Valentine was pregnant with her second baby and her daughter was the cutest kid she'd ever seen. Sofia never really thought about having kids but watching Anton play with his little niece did strange things to her heart. Luca seemed to fit right in with the guys. He even knew one of Val's husbands. Ace and he were both with the Gallos and had worked a few jobs together. Anton's mother was there and Sofia felt a pang of jealousy that he was surrounded by his family, all the people he loved and she might never have that again. Her father was dead and her mother was God only knew where, being held by the Marinos.

After introductions were made Valentine and her daughter, Maria and mother, Theresa whisked her into the kitchen to help get food ready. She grew up in a traditional Italian family and knew the score. They would have prepared enough food to feed an army and the women were the ones in the kitchen while the men went off to do their thing. But honestly, she felt a little out of sorts without Luca and Anton and wished she could just hang out with the guys. Being an only child Sofia was surrounded by boy cousins every Sunday afternoon when her extended family would come over for dinner. She wasn't really sure how to act around other women and since they were Anton's family she hoped like hell she didn't mess things up. She didn't know what she could and couldn't discuss with Valentine and her mother. Sofia would hate to say something that would hurt Anton so she opted to keep her mouth closed and her answers short and sweet.

"Are you hungry, Sofia?" Valentine asked. She shyly nodded hoping all their questions would require a yes or no answer. "I'm assuming you like Italian food?" Valentine smiled at her as she vigorously nodded her head.

Theresa stopped stirring a big pot of boiling macaroni and turned to her. "I know this isn't easy for you, Sofia. I can't imagine what you have been through these past few days. If we can help in any way, we'd like to." Valentine's mother seemed so earnest; she nearly broke down in tears. It had been so long since someone talked to her so sweetly she wasn't quite sure if she'd be able to speak past her emotions.

"Thank you, Mrs. Rossi," Sofia whispered past the lump in her throat. "I appreciate that."

"None of that Mrs. Rossi stuff," she scoffed. "You will call me Theresa. I have a feeling my Anton brought you here for a reason and we can just bypass all those silly formalities."

"Thank you, Theresa," Sofia said. "I take it Anton told you how we met then?" Sofia noticed the pang of sadness in Theresa's brown eyes and she was sure she had said something she shouldn't have.

"Unfortunately my Ani doesn't tell me much these days. He thinks I need protection from the Gallos but he forgets I was once a part of that family, even more so than him. My cousin is Isabella Gallo," she admitted. Sofia didn't hide her shock.

"Ani told us you escaped from the Marinos and you needed a safe place to stay but that's about it," Valentine said. Sofia knew this was one of those gray areas she was worried about sharing too much.

"Yes, Anton and Luca helped me to, um—get away from the family. I couldn't have done it without them." She paused, thinking back over her words trying to figure out if she said anything that would give away their true story. The last thing she wanted to do was tell Anton's mom or sister he and Luca bought her at an auction.

"Well, you are welcome to stay with me if you want," Theresa offered. Honestly, Sofia felt about ready to cry at such a sweet offer. Theresa Rossi reminded her so much of her own mother that Sofia couldn't hold back her sob.

"Thank you," she cried.

"Oh no, honey. Don't cry. I didn't mean to upset

you," Theresa said wrapping her arms around Sofia's body.

"It's not you. I just miss my own mother and you are all so nice," she wailed. Sofia felt like a fool for carrying on that way, but it was as if the weight of the past week had come crashing down on her and she couldn't control her outburst.

"What the hell happened, Ma?" Anton grouched, rounding the corner from the back porch where the men had gathered. He pulled Sofia into his arms and kissed her forehead. She willingly let him comfort her. Luca must have heard the commotion because he quickly joined them and framed her body with his own. Sofia was perfectly cocooned between their two big bodies and she had never felt so safe.

"Tell us what's wrong, baby," Luca pleaded. She was causing such a scene she knew there would be no going back from telling Anton's family what was going on between the three of them.

"I don't know what's wrong with me," she sobbed. "One minute I was fine and then the next minute your mom was being so nice to me that I couldn't control my tears," she cried.

"I'm sorry, Ani," Theresa said. "I simply told Sofia she was welcome to stay with me if she'd like."

Anton nodded, "Thanks Ma," he said. "But Sofia will be staying with Luca and me." The expression on Anton's face gave away his worry. Sofia knew she had messed things up for him with her irrational outburst and one word answers.

"We are—" Anton looked over at Luca and he shrugged as if he was silently telling him it was his call. "The three of us are together," Anton admitted.

"Well, that's great," Valentine gushed.

"I don't know why you wouldn't tell us, Ani. You know I've accepted Valentine's decision to be married to two men. I love Nick and Ace as if they were my own now. What made you hide this from me?" Theresa asked.

"It's a long and sorted story. How about we all sit down and I'll explain?" Anton sat at the head of the big table and pulled Sofia onto his lap not letting her protest, he wrapped his arms around her body. Luca sat to the side of them scooting his chair as close as possible to Anton, giving him his silent support. When the rest of the family sat down he cleared his throat and Sofia felt as though she was holding her own breath anticipating his next words.

"Luca and I are together too." Anton paused and looked at his mother and sister. Nick and Ace had joined them after putting little Maria down for her nap.

"You mean you're gay?" Nick asked. He didn't seem to be judging Anton, just asking a simple question as if it was no big deal.

"Bi," Anton admitted. "I'm with both Sofia and Luca." He looked back to his mother. "Say something Ma," he begged.

"I don't know why you wouldn't tell me, Ani. I don't care who you're with as long as you're happy. Keeping secrets is what nearly destroyed this family.

Your father kept secrets from us, not telling anyone about working to get out of the Gallo organization. It's what got him killed and you trapped in that awful family. I won't have you keeping secrets from us now. You can turn to us, lean on us and we'll never judge you," his mother said. "We're your family."

Anton nodded and Sofia could tell he was just barely keeping himself together. Luca must have noticed too because he reached for Anton's hand and smiled when he freely took it. "We're in trouble," Anton continued. "The Marinos are after Sofia and the Gallos are coming for Luca and me. We had nowhere else to go," he admitted.

"Well, you're home now and safe. I'm going to do everything I can to help you all. But you might as well tell Val and your Ma the rest, Anton," Nick said.

"I bid on Sofia at the Marino family's auction," Luca admitted. "It was all me, not Ani. He warned me not to but seeing her up on that stage being sold off like livestock, I couldn't take it. I've known Sofia since she was just a kid. She was friends with my little sister, Mila. I couldn't just let someone else have her," Luca admitted.

"I might have warned you against bidding on her but I wanted her too," Anton said. It was the first time he had said something like that. In the past twenty-four hours they had been together Sofia thought Luca was the only one who wanted her. She knew Anton promised to put her between the two of them but she just figured that had more to do with him wanting

Luca. She never would have guessed he wanted her from the start.

"Really?" she asked.

Anton pulled her in for a quick kiss. "Really," he admitted. "I was feeling all of the same crazy things Luca was when I saw you up on that stage, but I was afraid of what would happen if we went against Isabella's orders. She is not a very forgiving lady," Anton said. "Honestly, when Luca won you I felt relieved. I don't really know how else to explain it. I was happy you were going to leave that hell hole with us."

"Thank you, Anton," Sofia whispered. She had forgotten everyone else in the room and wrapped her arms around Anton's neck pulling him down to meet her lips. She liked the way he let her take control of the kiss. Sofia could feel Luca's eyes on them watching their every move and she had to admit it was hot knowing he was there.

Nick cleared his throat reminding her they weren't alone. "How about you guys pick this up later? I'm starving and we need to go over a few things before you head over to the safehouse," Nick said. Sofia giggled and shyly nodded.

"Sofia, why don't you help me and Ma in the kitchen and we will try not to make you cry again," Valentine crossed her heart making them all laugh. Anton let her up from his lap and Luca pulled her down onto his giving her the same attention Anton just had. She liked how different their kisses were. Anton's was sweet and full of passion while Luca kissed her as if he was going to devour her. Both kisses were hot and she couldn't wait to get to the safehouse to finish what they had all started.

"Ugg, give it a break," Ace teased. "We have business to discuss and then I have a pan of lasagna with my name on it." Luca pushed her up from his lap and she followed Val and Theresa into the kitchen.

Val sat in the corner of the room and rubbed her belly. "This little guy is going to be a football player," she said. Sofia had never really given much thought to having kids of her own but seeing little Maria playing with Anton and now Valentine talking about her new little one, made her wish for something she never wanted before.

"When are you due?" Sofia asked.

"In two months," Val said with a grimace. Sofia giggled at the face she made. "This pregnancy is so different than Maria's. I was constantly sick with her but this time I've had no morning sickness. He's just a ball of energy though, always moving. He's going to keep us on our toes, I'm sure of it."

"He'll be just like his fathers," Theresa said. She crossed the kitchen to sit next to Val and patted her belly. "She found out the sex of the baby this time. The guys drove her half-crazy not knowing if Maria was a boy or a girl." Theresa and Val laughed and Sofia felt that damn pang of jealousy again. She wondered if she would be able to have these same experiences with her mother someday. Sofia worried she would never see her mother again and that thought terrified her.

They sat in the kitchen and talked while Theresa finished cooking. Val was right; her mother had made enough to feed an entire army. They got everything on the table and when Theresa was finished she asked Sofia to go tell the guys dinner was ready. She found them all sitting in the family room talking in hushed tones. She couldn't help it; she tiptoed to the door and eavesdropped wanting to know what they were planning. A part of her worried the guys were going to try to protect her and keep her out of the loop but she wouldn't have it. Her father had done the same thing to her and her mother. She wanted to be a part of whatever they were planning especially if it involved her. Over the years she had gotten good at sneaking around and listening in on her parents' conversations. She gently put her ear to the door and could hear the murmur of male voices.

"Are you sure it's him?" She heard Luca whisper.

"Luca's right. How certain are you it's her father?" Anton asked.

"I'm one hundred percent sure it's her dad, guys." The voice sounded as if it was Nick's. His accent was a little different than the other guys, being from New York. "He was part of a large group of men who turned on the Marino family," Nick said.

"How could he do that to Sofia and her mother?" Luca questioned. "He just left them to pick up the pieces. What kind of man does that to his family?"

Sofia could feel her breath hitch. Were they talking about her father? How did Nick even know her dad if he was dead?

"I'm telling you guys—Vincent Marino is alive and well. He's in the city in a safe house until it's time for him to testify. He's been granted clemency for his testimony," Nick said. This time Sofia didn't mask her gasp. She barged into the room to find the four of them staring back at her.

"He's alive?" she asked. "My father is alive?"

Nick stood and slowly nodded. "He is, Sofia."

"He just left me and my mother," she whispered. Anton and Luca quickly flanked her sides and she wasn't sure if she wanted to lean into them for comfort or punch them for keeping her out of their meeting.

"Were you two going to tell me or just leave me in the dark?" She looked between Luca and Anton and knew her answer. They weren't going to tell her and that pissed her off.

"We just found out about it ourselves, Sofia," Anton said. "We would have checked the story out before telling you," he admitted.

"But we would have told you as soon as we had proof," Luca amended. Sofia wasn't sure what to believe. She wasn't sure who she could trust.

She turned to Nick, "Show me the proof," she ordered.

"It will take me a few days but I think I can arrange a meeting. I just need to clear it through my captain," Nick offered.

"Thank you," Sofia nodded and turned to walk out of the room. "Theresa said to tell you all dinner is ready," she said back over her shoulder. Sofia walked away from them not bothering to turn around and let them explain as they both begged her to. She wasn't ready to listen to any more from either of them and she wasn't sure she ever would be.

ANTON

Luca and Anton sat on either side of Sofia and he could feel the anger radiating off her small body. She was pissed at them both and she had every right to be. They had already broken their promise to be open and honest and discuss everything just the three of them. Instead, when it was time to discuss the next steps and make plans they shooed her off to the kitchen and kept her in the dark. He never wanted to be one of the traditional mafia Italian men he had grown to despise. He hated that way of life and hoped to find a woman or a partner who wanted to be his equal. Anton had finally found that in both Luca and Sofia and he was fucking everything up.

Sofia barely ate, pushing her food around on her plate and only taking bites when Theresa shot her a worried glance and Anton knew if he didn't fix things between them now he might never be able to.

"I'm sorry we didn't include you in our discussion, Sofia," he softly whispered.

Luca leaned into her body, "We fucked up," he admitted. "Will you please forgive us?" Sofia pressed her lips together and Anton was sure she wasn't going to give them an easy out.

"You two made me a promise and you broke it," she said. "How do I know this won't happen again? This is my life and I won't allow the two of you to push me aside and make decisions for me." Anton could feel his family's eyes on them although it was comical the way they all tried to pretend they weren't eavesdropping on their very private conversation.

"You don't know it won't happen again," Anton admitted. "You just met the two of us, but I can promise you that Luca and I will give you our word—we will include you in everything from now on."

Luca nodded his agreement, "Every decision we make," he swore. Luca crossed his heart for good measure and Sofia giggled at his exaggerated pout. Anton had to admit; Luca was the sexiest goofball he had ever met.

"Fine," Sofia agreed. "I'll hold you to your promise though—both of you." She winked at each of them and Anton wondered just which promise she was referring to. He hoped like hell it was their promise to make her theirs because it was all he could think about. He was counting down the minutes until he and Luca could get Sofia naked and show her just how much they would promise her. Anton was so close to having the two people he wanted most in the world; he just needed to get through their family dinner first.

Nick cleared his throat, "As soon as I have any news about your father, Sofia I will be in touch." Sofia nodded and thanked Nick. Anton just hoped like hell his brother-in-law wasn't setting her up for disappointment. She had already lost her father once. Giving her false hope and having to relive all those feelings of loss and betrayal if Nick was wrong might be devastating for her.

"Will you be sticking around then?" Valentine asked. Anton looked at his sister and saw all the hurt and pain he caused both her and his mother staring back at him. He knew leaving them the way he did must have been painful. He never meant to do that to either of them but there was no other way to keep his sister and her family safe. Anton knew his decision to work for the Gallo Family might cost him his family but he'd do it all over again if it meant they'd all be safe.

"Yeah," Anton said. "We can't risk being in Chicago right now—not with both families looking for us. I'm sure Isabella will have heard I've left the city by now. I'm not sure she fully bought my story about using Sofia to gain access to information about the Marinos. Honestly, I wouldn't put it past her to have her own agenda in letting me just walk out of our meeting."

"Like?" Ace questioned.

"Well, when I assured her Luca and I bought Sofia purely to gain tactical information to bring down the Marino family, she seemed skeptical. I was sure I wasn't going to walk out of the restaurant on my own. It didn't take much convincing to get Isabella to agree to give me some time to get the information she was looking for from Sofia. I know Isabella well enough to tell when she is up to something. I just don't know what it is this time," Anton admitted. He hated that Isabella might be plotting to hurt his family and he possibly gave her the tools to do so. Running to New York and putting Valentine's family in danger wasn't his finest decision, but it was his only way to ensure Luca and Sofia's safety.

"So we'll be seeing more of you?" his mother hopefully asked.

"Yes Ma, I promise." Anton knew better than to make his mother such an oath, but the hope in her eyes made it damn near impossible to give her any other answer.

"Listen, I hate to be the bearer of bad news here but I need to get you guys to the safe house. You will most likely have a long day tomorrow answering questions," Nick said. Sofia winced at the mention of being interrogated and Luca pulled her against his big body wrapping a protective arm around her.

"We'll get through this together, honey," he promised. "Ani and I will take care of you." Anton smiled at them both. They were already becoming a team and they hadn't even been together but a couple of days. He wondered if they were jumping into the deep end too soon, but every moment he spent with Sofia and Luca felt right.

"I'm ready whenever you are, Nick," Anton said. "Will we be able to get a few necessities? I was able to get the clothes we are wearing but that is about all we have. None of us could go home to pack since we were being watched."

"Can you shop online? I'll give you my credit card to use and you can order everything you need and have it overnighted," Nick offered.

"So, we won't be free to come and go as we please?" Luca questioned.

Nick held up his hands as if defending himself. "I never said that. But, for your own personal safety I suggest you stay in and hidden from public eye. I know you think you are safe here, but you aren't. The Marino and Gallo families both have eyes and ears in New York. They will be watching for you to make an appearance here knowing your family is in the city, Anton."

Anton agreed they would stay out of the public eye. The last thing he wanted to do was attract unwanted attention. "There will be a plain clothed undercover detective placed at the house. He's there to protect you, not keep you under lock and key. You three came to me willingly. Nothing about this will be forced or coerced," Nick said.

"Thanks for that," Anton said. "We will help as much as we can. Our goal is to bring down as many families as possible. Between the three of us we should be able to provide you with a good deal of information to do just that."

"Great," Nick said. "Let's head out and get you three settled. I'm sure you must be tired from your trip." Anton had to admit he was anything but tired. He was feeling overly emotional at seeing his family again. And he was itching to get his hands on Luca and Sofia. Getting to the safehouse seemed like the best fucking idea he had heard all day. The sooner he got there the sooner he could make Luca and Sofia his.

THEY FOLLOWED Nick to the safehouse and he introduced the police detective assigned to them. After the grand tour of the little brownstone they were going to call home for the unforeseeable future, Nick told them he'd be back the next morning at nine. Anton knew he would be bringing in most of his station to question them. He just hoped like hell the three of them were ready.

They were finally alone and he could feel the uncertainty and nervousness humming through the air; the three of them crowded in the small master bedroom he hoped they would be sharing. He hated how the three of them were back to feeling shy after last night's admission of wanting each other. Anton just needed to remind Luca and Sofia what they promised and he knew just how to do that.

"Luca, come here," Anton ordered. Luca might have been older than he was, but they were both used to Anton calling the shots. Luca liked to be bold when it came to taking what he wanted from him, but seeing him shy and unsure of himself gave Anton the courage to take control of the situation. Anton would have no problem playing alpha, it was how he usually liked things.

Luca obeyed Anton, turning back to face him. "Kiss me," Anton ordered. Luca shyly smiled at Sofia as if he knew exactly what Anton was trying to do. She liked to watch the two of them together and Anton loved the way her breath hitched at his mere command to Luca. He was sure Sofia would be just as compliant once she had her turn with him.

"Yes sir," Luca whispered against his lips. Luca sealed his mouth over Anton's and he all but consumed him with the powerful give and take of their kiss. Anton loved how Luca never seemed to hold back with him. Whenever he kissed him Luca gave him all the passion Anton saw in his eyes whenever they were alone together. How he ignored the signs for so long he had no idea. Wanting Luca was as easy as breathing for him and Anton wasn't sure he would ever be able to turn off his growing desires for him.

They broke their kiss and looked over to where Sofia was intently watching them. Her breathing had hitched and Anton could tell by her pink cheeks she was completely turned on by what she had just seen. "You like watching us together, don't you, Princess?"

Sofia shyly nodded, "Yes," she whispered. "I think it's hot," she admitted. Luca smiled and pulled her against his body pausing as if he was waiting for Anton to tell him what to do next. It was a heady feeling knowing someone like Luca Gallo would let him call the shots. It made him hot and a whole lot turned on knowing the power Luca was gifting him with.

"Kiss our girl, Luca," he ordered. Luca didn't hesitate. He gently nipped and licked his way into her mouth and Anton loved her breathy little sighs and moans Luca elicited from her. He needed to taste her, touch her and God, he wanted to fuck her—but he needed to remember this was going to be her first time. He and Luca were going to have to be gentle with her and give her time to adjust to being theirs. He framed her body with his own, effectively trapping Sofia between the two of them.

"My turn," he said, turning her into his body and slamming his mouth against hers. He wasn't gentle like Luca was with her. He felt consumed with a need and desire like he had never felt before.

Anton reluctantly broke their kiss leaving them both panting. "I need you both naked," he commanded. Luca smiled and stripped out of his t-shirt and Anton couldn't keep his hands from Luca's body. He was pure muscle and his tattoos that covered most of his right arm, shoulder and chest turned Anton on. He'd seen Luca without his shirt when they were working out but this was different. Luca was giving himself to Anton and seeing him naked in person was better than any of the fantasies that plagued his nightly dreams.

"So fucking hot, babe," Anton growled. He unfastened Luca's jeans and pulled them down his thick thighs, loving the fact he was completely bare underneath. It was so like Luca not to wear anything under his pants, it shouldn't have surprised him but it did. The sight of Luca's cock springing free as Anton pulled his jeans down made him groan. Anton sunk to his knees and teasingly looked up Luca's body before sucking his hard shaft into his mouth. Anton licked and sucked Luca's cock knowing he was taking him to the very edge of sanity because he felt the exact same way.

"Ani," Luca hissed. Anton released his cock and kissed his way up Luca's body. "Such a tease," Luca whispered.

"Your turn, Princess," Anton offered. He turned to where Sofia stood watching them. "I need to taste you too, baby." Sofia's soft moan escaped her parted lips and he knew she was just as turned on as he was.

"Yes, Ani please," she begged. Hearing her call him by his nickname did strange things to his heart. It was the first time she let her defenses down and called him that and he wanted more from her. He wanted her underneath his body panting out his fucking name, but that would happen soon enough.

He tugged her shirt up over her head loving how she wasn't wearing a bra. He nipped and sucked his way down her body paying special attention to her sensitive nipples. She moaned out her pleasure and he couldn't wait to see and taste the rest of her. Anton pulled down her leggings and Luca pulled her back against his body kissing his way into her mouth as he plucked her taut nipples. She was on edge and this time

Anton planned on letting her fall. He wanted to see her come undone for him—for them both. He wanted to taste her release as she came all over his tongue. Anton worked her leggings and panties the rest of the way down her curvy body leaving her completely bare for them both to play with.

"You are so fucking beautiful, Sofia," Luca praised. She shyly shook her head as if she didn't believe him.

"He's right, baby. You are gorgeous," Anton agreed. "And you're ours," he said.

"Yes," she promised. "Please make me yours—both of yours." Anton loved how she so freely submitted to them asking them both for what she wanted. It was all he hoped for. He sunk to his knees and parted her wet folds, licking his way into her pussy. Sofia's body quivered reminding Anton this was all so new to her.

"Do you like what he's doing to you baby?" Luca asked. Sofia shivered and nodded.

"Yes," she moaned. "Please don't stop," she begged. Anton smiled up at her and dipped his head back between her legs lapping at her pussy, loving the way she ground against his face taking her pleasure from him. Sofia quickly fell over the edge of pleasure coating Anton's tongue with her release. He couldn't seem to get enough of her body as she writhed against him, riding out her orgasm. Luca held her body against his helping Sofia to stay upright.

"Thank you, Ani," she panted leaning into Luca's chest.

"That was so fucking hot," Luca whispered. Anton

knew he was prolonging his torture but he couldn't help it. He wanted them both so much.

"Our turn," Sofia sassed pulling Anton's shirt up his body. Judging from the wicked way she and Luca were staring him down as if he was their next meal he was about to get just as good as he gave—and he couldn't wait.

LUCA

Luca helped Ani shuck out of his clothes loving the way he responded to every touch, kiss and bite. Luca couldn't believe he was finally going to have the man he had wanted for so long. He wanted Anton since their first week together but wasn't sure if Ani would turn him away. All the signs were there—the way Ani looked at him and the electricity he felt every time their bodies accidently touched. It was almost too much to dream of Ani being his in that way.

Being bi was never a problem for Luca. He never hid the fact from his family or friends that he liked both men and women. His parents always seemed to be okay with who he was and never really made a big deal about it. Hearing how Ani never told his family about that side of himself made Luca sad. Anton had to pretend to be something he wasn't and that thought pained Luca. He had fallen in love with Ani from the start and knowing he lived with the constant pressure of having to hide such a big part of who he was, must have taken its toll on his friend. Hearing him admit to his family today that he was bi and in a relationship with both Luca and Sofia made him so damn happy. Luca tried not to make a big deal out of it but it was. And now they had found the perfect woman to fit between the two of them Luca wasn't sure how he had gotten so lucky.

"Luca," Anton growled as he leaned back against his body. Anton faced Sofia and Luca had to admit watching the two of them together was hot. Luca framed Ani's back and wrapped his arms around his big body. He grabbed Anton's cock loving the way he seemed to lose a little of his control when he thrust into Luca's hands taking what he needed from him.

"Yes like that," Anton moaned. "Please," he begged. Sofia smiled and winked at him over Anton's shoulder and he was sure their princess had some naughty plans for their guy.

"I think I'd like to taste you, Ani," she whispered.

"Yes," Anton hissed.

"Um, I've never done this before," she admitted and Luca's heart stuttered. He forgot just how new this all was to Sofia.

"How about I teach you, baby?" Luca asked. She smiled back at him and enthusiastically nodded her agreement causing him to laugh.

They both kneeled in front of Anton and he was

sure his guy wouldn't have things any other way. Ani liked being in charge and Luca liked it when Anton told him what to do. He always liked to be topped but he'd never admit it. Anton seemed to sense just what he needed so far.

"Wrap your hand around the base of his cock and cup his balls," Luca ordered. Sofia obeyed. He had to admit topping their girl felt pretty damn natural to him. She seemed to be a natural sub and he and Anton were going to have fun training her to be theirs. "Good girl," he praise and she gifted him with another of her sexy smiles.

"Now what?" she asked. Luca could see Anton was barely holding it together. They both needed to get off and if Luca had his way he'd find his release deep inside Sofia.

"Now suck the head into your mouth. Take as much of him as you can and breathe through your nose." Sofia did and when she was about to gag she released him. Anton's frustrated groan filled the room and Luca couldn't help himself, he took over for her to show Sofia what he knew Anton would want.

He sucked Anton's shaft into his mouth, letting his tongue swirl around the head of his cock, and God he tasted good. Luca worked Ani's cock deep into his throat and swallowed around him. He could tell Ani was close, but he wanted Sofia to finish him off.

"Like that," he said. "Now you try." She nodded and sucked Ani back into her mouth and he thrust in a little further taking over for her. Anton held her hair back so Luca could watch her cheeks hollow out ever time Anton slid in and out of her mouth. It was the hottest fucking thing he had ever seen.

"Yes, Princess," Anton praised. "I'm going to come." Anton tried to pull out of Sofia's mouth but she wouldn't allow it, sucking him in deeper. She swallowed around his cock and that was all Ani needed to find his release. Their girl took everything Anton gave her and licked his shaft clean.

"Perfect job, honey," Luca praised as she released Anton's cock from her mouth.

"Your turn," she teased wrapping her hands around Luca's cock. He knew if she got her sweet lips around his dick he'd never get inside of her. He looked up to Anton silently pleading for permission to take her and Ani nodded as if knowing just what he was asking.

"Can Luca be your first, baby?" Anton asked. Luca knew a part of Ani wanted to order her to get up on the bed and spread her legs for them, but they needed to remember she was a virgin.

Sofia looked between the two of them as if not understanding the question. "I thought you would both be my first?" she asked.

Anton chuckled at her confusion. "We can't both take your virginity, baby," he said. "Since you and Luca have known each other longer he should be the one to take it." Luca had no claim to Sofia and he loved how Anton wanted him to be the one to take her, but he worried he might be too rough with her. He felt his own breath hitch while they waited her out for an answer. Sofia finally nodded.

"Yes, I'd like for Luca to be my first," she admitted. "When I was a kid I used to dream about you making me yours, Luca. Please," she begged.

"Thank you, Sofia," he whispered. "I'm worried I'll hurt you though."

"It's okay," she said. "It's going to hurt either way. I want it to be you." She wrapped her arms around his neck and pulled him down for a kiss. She was giving him a gift and there would be no way he'd be able to tell her no. Not now—he wanted her too much.

She broke their kiss and looked at him expecting him to be able to answer. It was going to be damn near impossible for him to make one syllable words let alone sentences. He was completely on edge. Luca backed her up to the bed and Anton joined her. Luca loved how the three of them seemed to be in this together. He knew Anton would have his back no matter how nervous he was about taking Sofia.

She reached her arms out to him and Luca covered her body with his own, feeling the bed dip with their weight. He pulled Anton in for a hard kiss loving the way Sofia watched the two of them.

"My turn," she said. Sofia pulled Luca down for a long passionate kiss and wrapped her hands around his shaft guiding it through her drenched folds. Luca hissed out his breath at just how good she felt.

"Please," she whimpered. "Take me, Luca," she

moaned. He couldn't help himself he thrust into her, balls deep, only stopping when she cried out.

"I'm so sorry, baby," he groaned. Luca tried to hold as still as humanly possible knowing she would need time to adjust to being filled by him. He had never been with a virgin in his life; not even when he lost his own virginity. This was a first for him too and he wasn't quite sure what to do next.

Anton peppered her face with soft kisses whispering praises as Sofia tried to work through the pain. She smiled up at him, "I think I'm alright now, Luca." He was still afraid to move for fear of hurting her again. He felt as though he was fucking everything up and self-doubt clouded his judgement.

"Move, please," she begged. Luca hesitantly pulled free from her body and slipped back into her core. She met him thrust for thrust as if she needed exactly what he wanted to give to her. Luca tried to be gentle, but he wasn't sure it was even a possibility.

"Fuck you feel so good, baby," he admitted. He knew he wasn't going to last much longer and he wanted her with him. "Help her please, Ani," he begged. Anton's smirk told Luca he knew exactly what he needed to do. Anton sucked her nipple into his mouth and snaked his hand down between their bodies finding her clit. Luca could feel Anton's fingers rubbing her sensitive nub and her greedy pussy clenched around his cock, milking his orgasm out of him. Sofia followed him over moaning out both of their names and he had never heard a sweeter sound. It was as if she was confirming she was theirs and Luca knew he would never be able to let either of them go. Anton and Sofia were his now whether they knew it or not. They each owned a piece of his heart and he'd never be whole again without them both.

SOFIA

Sofia woke the next morning cuddled between Luca and Anton's big bodies. She had never felt safer and more cared for in her life. Being an only child, Sofia was often lonely. That was why she relied on friends like Mila to have play dates with. She had always regretted her crass decision to discard one of her best friends simply over a boy. Although Luca didn't exactly qualify as a boy. By the time Sofia kicked Mila to the curb, Luca was a grown man. She almost wanted to pinch herself. It felt like a dream the way she was cuddled against his body now.

The whole night felt like a dream with the way Ani and Luca shared her. She would have never been one to believe she would end up with not one but two of the sexiest men she had ever met. She was quickly losing her heart to them both and that thought scared the shit out of her. What if she was just a way for the two of them to connect. They both admitted to being bi—what if the woman between them was interchangeable? Both guys said they wanted her and she was theirs, but her self-doubt and inner voice were both screaming at her that she would never be good enough for them. She was so young and naive and up until last night had zero experience with men.

Sure, Sofia had the occasional boyfriend in high school, but as soon as the boy found out who her father was they found some excuse to end the relationship. Truthfully, no boy had ever gotten past second base with her and now that she had Luca and Anton in her life she wanted to explore and learn all she could. If her time with them was going to be just temporary she wanted to take full advantage of their bossy natures and walk away fully sated and ready to be the woman she was becoming and not the scared little mouse her father had raised her to be. Sofia wanted to be free to make her own choices and not have to look over her shoulder every few seconds. Anton and Luca were giving her all those things and she would be eternally grateful to them both.

"Hey, sleepy head," Luca whispered kissing his way down the column of her neck. "How are you feeling this morning?" Sofia wrinkled her nose assessing the dull ache in her core from being well used by the both of them throughout the night.

"Alright," she lied. Luca chuckled against her skin igniting the same fire she felt for the two of them all night long. It was crazy the way her body responded to them both. She wondered if she would ever tire of them touching and kissing her. Sofia had a feeling she already knew the answer to her question and that would make them leaving her all the more painful.

"How about I run you a bath and you can soak for a while? It will help you feel better." Sofia pouted at him and he laughed again.

"I was hoping you would join me," she whispered.

"No, sweetheart. I have a feeling Ani and I were a little rough with you last night." He smirked at her and she couldn't help her giggle. Honestly, she thought they were perfect, but since she had no prior experience to base her opinion, she kept it to herself.

"I'd love a bath then," she admitted. "Thank you."

Anton rolled over and cuddled into her other side. "You two are the loudest whispers I've ever heard."

"Sorry," Sofia whispered and then giggled.

"It's alright. I guess we should get up and get moving. They entire NYPD will be here in a couple hours and we will need to be ready," Anton said. Sofia had all but forgotten they were going to be questioned this morning. The guys helped her to forget all the bad stuff and only concentrate on them. She knew sooner or later reality would resurface and she would have to face all the bad shit that happened to her but she was hoping for a little more of a reprieve.

"Sorry, Princess but we won't be able to hide forever," Anton said as if able to read her mind.

"I know, but I wish we could stay just like this at least for a while longer," Sofia said.

"We will have plenty of time for more of this," Luca said, palming her sensitive breasts.

"And more of this," Anton growled, kissing his way into her mouth.

"Good," she whispered against Ani's lips. "I'd like that," she admitted. Luca got out of bed and she instantly regretted agreeing to a bath. She'd rather he stay just where he was, but Sofia knew it was time to face the music.

Anton grew quiet and she worried she had done or said something wrong. She and Luca seemed to have a connection knowing each other from when they were younger. Anton and she didn't have that, but Sofia was hoping they were building something between the three of them which would bind them together.

"You know we meant everything we said last night, Sofia," Anton whispered. "We want you and that isn't going to change."

Sofia nodded but she was still listening to those quiet voices in her head; the ones that told her she wasn't good enough for either of them. That they only wanted her because she was convenient and easy. They were the same voices that whispered that when the guys got tired of her they would just kick her to the curb and move on. It was as if Anton could see her self-doubt creeping in and he seemed determined to erase it from existence.

Anton pulled her on top of his body so she straddled his cock. She gasped when she realized he was hard and ready. Sofia couldn't help but rub her sensitive folds against him as if inviting him to take what he wanted from her.

"No baby, you must be sore," Anton said, his voice hoarse with need.

"I need you, Ani," she begged lowering her wet pussy down onto his erection taking all of him. She leaned down and kissed his mouth silently asking him to give her what she needed. Anton seemed to understand what she was asking him for, giving her complete control over his body. She rode his cock loving the way he touched her body. He was so gentle and loving she could almost hear him saying those three little words to her. The words no one had ever said to her, not even her own parents.

Anton reached between their bodies and rubbed her sensitive clit until she found her release growling out his name as she rode his cock. Ani quickly followed her over finding his own release, whispering her name like a prayer. She was sure she would never get enough of him—of either of them.

Ani pulled her back down to lay next to him and she noticed Luca was standing in the corner of the room watching the two of them. He smiled at her and winked. "I love watching you two together," he easily admitted. When the guys first asked her to be theirs she worried there would be jealousy, especially if they spent one on one time together. But there didn't seem to be any animosity between the guys and she sure as hell didn't mind when they were together. Watching them with each other was beautiful. Sofia could tell they had formed a bond and she'd even go as far as to guess they had already fallen for each other, but they just weren't ready to admit it yet.

Luca crossed to room and stood over the rumpled bed, "Come on, baby. Let's get you into that bath. Ani and I are going to take a shower and then we'll make you some breakfast," he offered. Sofia had to admit the sound of a hot bath and food sounded too good to be true. She was starving since not eating much the night before.

"That sounds perfect," she squealed as Luca lifted her into his arms cradling her against his body. She wrapped her arms around his neck and buried her face into his chest. She could get used to being treated this way. Everyone around her always assumed she was a princess, but when she was home that couldn't be further from the truth. Her father was never home and her mother seemed to be in a constant state of depression, often masking it with alcohol. She hated how her mom had to suffer from her father's life choices—they both had. Now, she was finally free from the Marino family, but her poor mother was still their captive and she would do anything within her power to change that. Sofia was afraid it might be too late to do anything for her mother though. The family would have taken Sofia's betrayal out on her mother and she feared the worst had happened.

Luca helped her into the warm soapy water and she sunk down to let the heavenly suds envelope her body. He was right, she was a little sore and the warm water helped to sooth her aching muscles. "Thank you," she stuttered.

"You alright, baby?" Luca asked, as if he could read her sudden change in mood. How could she tell him she was worried about her mother without sounding ungrateful to him and Anton for rescuing her from that hell hole?

"I'm a little worried about my mom," she admitted. Sofia wouldn't hide from Luca or Ani; she promised them her trust and honesty and expected the same from them. She wouldn't settle for anything less or give them less in return. "I feel like a coward for running away and leaving her there. I should have never left Chicago. What if I could have helped her? I won't be able to live with myself if my actions caused her any pain or suffering," Sofia sobbed.

Anton stood in the doorway and she had to admit she could get used to them both being gloriously naked all the time. "We will do everything in our power to make sure your mother is safe, Sofia," Anton promised. "Nick has already been in touch with his contact in the Marino family and as of last night he received word your mother is still alive but they are keeping her under lock and key. He believes they are hoping to use her as bait to get you back. You were a big payday for them and they will stop at nothing to get to you."

"That can't be the only reason they want Sofia back," Luca said. "They have to want something else. How many times can they sell her off as a virgin bride?" he questioned.

Sofia laughed, "Well, apparently the answer is once. Because I won't be able to claim that title after last night." She smiled up at them and Luca looked as if he was unsure whether she was joking or not. Anton looked just a serious and she couldn't help her laugh. "I was kidding guys. Seriously, you two need to lighten up some. I was the one they kidnapped and held against her will. I was the one they sold off, marketing me as a virgin bride and yet you two are the ones acting as if you are butt hurt about what happened—to me."

Anton sat down on the side of the tub and rinsed her hair. He worked some shampoo into her long brown curls and Sofia had to admit his fingers felt like magic massaging her scalp. "We are acting this way because we care about you, Sofia," Anton all but whispered. "We won't ever let the Marino family touch you again. You agreed to be ours and we take that very seriously." She looked up at Luca and he nodded his agreement.

"Ani's right, baby. I won't every let them near you again. We just need your promise you won't go off and do something stupid like trying to rescue your mother. You need to trust us to protect you and we will do everything in our power to help get her back," Luca promised.

"Thank you," she whispered.

"Always, Princess," Anton said, rinsing the shampoo from her hair.

Luca turned on the shower and she sat back in the tub and watched the two of them in the adjoining glass enclosed shower together. She would never get tired of seeing them so freely touch and kiss each other. This world was so new to her but it was quickly becoming her new normal. Sofia already had come to depend on both Luca and Anton and she worried when this all came to an end she'd find herself alone and heartbroken, but she wasn't willing to walk away from either of them.

ANTON

Anton had spent most of the morning wrapped up in two people he was beginning to fall for. After they ate breakfast and did some online shopping Nick showed up with what seemed to be most of the NYPD. Anton hated seeing the fear in Sofia's eyes every time he looked across the room to where another detective questioned her. They were being interrogated separately and he wished he could go to her and pull her into his arms to tell her everything was going to be alright. When he asked his brother-in-law for help he never imagined the three of them would be put through such vigorous questioning. A part of him felt as though he had let Luca and Sofia down, but he also knew he did exactly what he had to do to keep them both safe.

"We're almost finished here, Anton," Nick promised. "I know this is tough, especially watching your girl having to go through all of this and not being able to help her. I felt the same way when my captain insisted on questioning your sister and Ace. You all might have information that could help us bring down two major crime families in Chicago and that would be huge." Anton nodded knowing that Nick was right. He just hated how they were being put through the paces.

"I get it, man. I appreciate all of your help, Nick," Anton whispered.

"No problem, man," Nick said. "That's what family is for. Your mother and sister are so glad you're here, Anton."

"I know. I just hope I don't let anyone down is all," Anton admitted. "Sofia is worried about her mother. Is there any way you can find out how she is?" Anton knew Sofia would want an update on her mother and he was hoping any news might calm her nerves. The last thing he or Luca needed was for her to take off and play the hero. She already felt responsible for her mother being held by the Marino family. There was no telling what lengths she might go to in order to secure her mother's freedom. He made a deal with the devil herself to make sure his mother and Valentine were safe from the Gallos.

"I will make some calls. If everything goes according to plan my team will be in place by tonight. We plan on raiding the warehouse where you and Luca found Sofia. Illegal trafficking rings are a big target for us and if her mother is being held there we'll find her and keep her safe," Nick promised.

"Thanks, man," Anton muttered. "What about her

father?" he asked. Nick sighed and he was sure he wasn't going to like what he was about to hear.

"I'm still working on everything but it looks like he got out, man—he's alive," Nick whispered. Anton hated how this news would blow Sofia's world completely apart, but he wouldn't tell her anything until he had more concrete evidence from his brother-in-law. His girl had already been through enough.

A FEW HOURS LATER, they were done with questioning and Anton wasn't sure what to do next. They made some dinner and he loved the easy rhythm they found when the three of them worked together. It was as if they had been together for years and not just a couple of days. Anton listened as Luca teased Sofia about things she used to do when they were kids and he had to admit he thought he might be jealous knowing the two of them had a shared past, but he wasn't. He knew Luca's past relationship with Sofia was mostly why she trusted them both. He loved the way the two teased and taunted each other and hoped one day he and Sofia would have the same easiness to their relationship.

"And then, there was that one time I was outside working on my first car. I must have been about twenty and you were what—ten?" Luca asked. From the mischievous smile Sofia flashed him she knew just what he was going to say.

"Yes," she giggled. "And you had your shirt off," she added.

"Yep," Luca proudly exclaimed puffing out his broad chest. "You wandered out into the garage leaving Mila to play with her Barbies or whatever and you stood by the hood of my car gawking at me as though you had never seen a guy with his shirt off before."

"I hadn't," Sofia admitted. "I remember thinking you were the most handsome boy I had ever seen and I believe you had this tattoo, right here." She pointed to Luca's upper arm where the Gallo's mark prominently covered his bicep. It was a tattoo every member of the family was forced to have. Anton had his own, but he really didn't pay much attention to it.

"I couldn't take my eyes off of you," Sofia admitted.

"And I thought you were the nosiest brat I had ever met," Luca teased.

"What about now?" she questioned.

Luca looked her up and down his gaze lingering as he looked over her curves. "Now, I think you're the sexiest woman I've ever laid eyes on," he growled. Sofia gifted Luca with her shy smile and went up on her tiptoes to kiss his mouth.

"And you, Ani?" she asked, a little breathless from Luca's kiss. Anton couldn't help himself; he pulled Sofia against his body and kissed his way down her neck.

"I agree with our guy but I'm feeling at a bit of a disadvantage here," Anton admitted. "You two have a history that you and I don't share. I wish I knew you a little better."

Sofia wrapped her arms around his shoulders and he loved the way she cuddled into his arms. "What would you like to know, Ani?" she asked. "I'm an open book."

"Well, how about your middle name," Anton asked.

"Maria," she said. Anton smiled at hearing how she shared the same name as his great-grandmother.

"How about your birthday?" he asked.

"September twenty-third," she offered. "I'll be twenty-two this fall," she admitted.

"Do you have any brothers or sisters?" Anton asked. Sofia shook her head and he wanted to kick himself for asking the question. He hated the sadness in her eyes and he wished he could take it back. "You don't have to answer that, Sofia," Anton offered.

"No it's fine," she said. "I'm an only child and well, it was lonely growing up without anyone to talk to. My father worked crazy hours for the family and he wasn't around a whole lot. My mother was usually in her own world. She was sad and drank a lot to mask her depression. I grew up knowing how to take care of myself from a very young age." Luca crowded up behind her and wrapped his arms around her and Anton.

"I'm so sorry, Sofia," Luca whispered. "I never knew you were going through all of that. I should have been there for you. I could have done more if I had known."

"No, Luca," she said. "I was just a kid and not your responsibility. Looking back now I see my loneliness was why I liked being at your house with your family. There was always so many kids around and your home seemed like such a happy place."

Luca nodded, "It was."

"I was so stupid," she moaned. "I was so fixated on trying to act cool around you I never realized I was hurting Mila. When you moved out and got your own place I even stopped asking her to hang out. She probably hates me for the way I treated her," Sofia said.

"No," Luca said. "Mila would never hate you, Sofia. At one point you two were best friends. When the time is right, tell her what you just told us and I know my little sister will forgive you," Luca promised. Sofia smiled up at them through her tears and nodded.

"I will. Thank you, Luca," she said. "I don't know what I would do without either of you." Sofia wrapped her arms around each of their waists and snuggled into their bodies. Anton loved how she seemed to need them as much as they wanted her.

"How about we have some dinner and then we can watch a movie or something," Anton offered.

"Will we have to be here long?" Sofia asked.

"I have no idea, honey," Luca said. "We won't take any chances with you, Sofia," he said. Anton had to agree the last thing either of them wanted was to put her in danger again and they would do whatever they had to in order to keep her safe. Anton worried he was going to have to come clean and share the news about

133

her father with Sofia and Luca, but he didn't want them worrying until he had more evidence. Nick promised to call with news by the morning and Anton planned on keeping Luca and Sofia extra busy until then. He was sure he could come up with some creative ways to kill time until the next morning.

LUCA

Luca spent the night lying next to the two people who were quickly becoming his whole world, tossing and turning worrying about what their next move would be. He knew they wouldn't be able to hide from the families forever. The three of them would garner quite a bounty from both families and sooner or later someone would catch up with them trying to collect. He gave up on sleep just before dawn and carefully pulled himself free from Ani and Sofia's warm bodies.

He wished he could hit the gym or go for a run to work off some of the extra stress he felt but that would be a stupid move. They needed to keep their heads down and stay out of the public eye, careful not to garner any unwanted attention.

Reminiscing with Sofia about their past made him miss his parents. It had been almost a year since he had seen them. They didn't make it back to Chicago during the last winter season due to his father's failing health.

It was just too much for his dad to travel all the way to Chicago from Florida. He did better in the warmer weather and he couldn't bring himself to ask either of his parents to risk coming north to visit. He made them promises he would make the trip down to Florida but he never kept them. Luca always found an excuse not to visit usually involving the family and work, but he knew his reasoning went much deeper than that. He was afraid to see his father. Luca hated how his father's health had declined so quickly and a part of him didn't want to see that side of his dad. The other reason he feared facing his father was Luca felt like he failed him in some way. He hated that he had been demoted in the family after fucking up and disobeying Isabella's orders. He just couldn't carry out her plans of hurting innocent people just because they were facing hard times and couldn't pay. His father wouldn't understand he was following his conscious and that meant more to Luca than obeying the family. His dad was old school and he wouldn't understand going against the family no matter what the reasoning was behind Luca's decision to do so. News of what he and Anton did, buying Sofia and then sneaking out of the city, would have reached his father by now and he couldn't face his dad's disappointment.

Out of all his sisters Luca was closest to his youngest one, Mila. He decided to take his chances with her since he knew she would be the most likely to understand. As the baby of the family, Mila had a special bond with both of their parents. If anyone could plead his case for him it would be Mila. He just hoped

Sofia wasn't right about his sister hating her. Mila might not like that he was with Sofia now and that might hurt his chances of her helping him.

Luca pulled his cell from his pocket and found Mila's number. He knew it was early but he needed to talk to her, wanting to hear her voice. A part of him worried the Gallos might go after his sisters to get to him. He just needed to make sure they were all safe. Mila moved to California a while back and it was just after midnight there. He hoped he'd still catch her up since his little sister was a night owl.

"Lo," her groggy voice answered and Luca inwardly cursed knowing he had woken her.

"Hey, Sis," he murmured. "Did I wake you?" He already knew the answer to his question but he still asked.

"Yes, Luca, you fucking woke me. Why the hell are you calling me?" she whined. "Fuck," she yelled into the phone. "Tell me Mom and Dad are alright," she ordered.

"Yeah, I'm assuming they are. That's not why I'm calling really." He sighed into the line knowing he was about to spill his guts and that might not end well for him. Plus, he might be putting his sister in danger and he hated that idea.

"Then what's up?" she asked.

"You remember Sofia Marino?" he asked.

"Yes. She was supposed to be my best friend, but I think she only hung around me to get to you," Mila groused. He knew his sister had guessed correctly, but he didn't want to fuel her anger if she still felt any towards Sofia.

"Yeah, well it's a damn long story but we are together." Luca winced at the string of curses that came out of his little sister. She had always been creative when it came to her use of the English language.

"Fuck, Luca. I thought you were trying to get with your partner, Anton or whatever his name is," she said.

"Um, well—I am with him too," he admitted. This whole conversation wasn't going as planned and a part of him wanted to just end the call. But he knew Mila would just pester him until he spilled the details.

"Tell me you aren't two timing them, Luca. That never ends well for anyone," she said. Luca wondered if his little sister was speaking from experience and he wanted to question her but he'd save that for another time.

"No, I'm not cheating on either of them. The three of us are together and well, I'm happy," he said. "Sofia's father turned against the Marinos and in retaliation they took her and sold her off in a trafficking auction." He hated having to tell Mila about the dirty parts of his job. He wanted to keep her pure and as far away from family business as humanly possible; but her last name was Gallo and that made her a part of his world—like it or not.

Mila gasped into the line. "You mean they were selling off women?" she asked.

"Yeah," Luca whispered. "Anton and I were sent in by the Gallos to get intel. But when I saw Sofia I just couldn't leave her there. The thought of someone else buying her and doing God knows what with her—I just couldn't let that happen," he said.

"No, of course you couldn't. You are a good man, Luca," Mila said.

"Thanks, Sis," Luca said around the lump in his throat. No one had ever called him that before and hearing his little sister believed in him did strange things to his heart. "We got Sofia out of there but disobeyed family orders. Now, the three of us are on the run and both the Marinos and Gallos are looking for us."

"Fuck, Luca," Mila spat. "What can I do to help?"

"Can you call Mom and Dad to make sure they are safe? I don't think this will affect them but you never know. Isabella Gallo won't be happy I've disobeyed her again. At some point she might try to get to my family and it's too dangerous for me to contact anyone else," he admitted.

"Yes, I'm going to fly to Florida at the end of the week to see them. I had some time off from school and I thought I could give Mom a break," she said. "Dad's being a handful." Luca smiled at the thought of his dad giving his mom a hard time. That woman was a saint in his book for putting up with everything she did over the years.

"I'm sorry I can't help with him," Luca said.

"I'll keep you updated and let the others know what's going on. Don't worry Luca, we all have your back on this," Mila promised.

"Thanks," he whispered.

"And—" he could hear the hesitation in Mila's voice and he hated she was censoring anything she wanted to say to him. They were always completely open and honest with each other and he needed that from her now.

"Just say it, Mila," he ordered.

"Well, I was just going to say I'm glad you have found two people who make you happy, Luca. You deserve it," she said.

"Thanks, Sis," he said. "Keep in touch. Love you," he murmured.

"Love you too, Luca," she said and ended the call. Luca wasn't sure how he was going to keep his family safe but he'd do whatever he had to. Now that vow included his newest family, Sofia and Anton. He'd do whatever he needed to in order to keep them both safe —even risk his own life.

SOFIA

It had been almost a month since the three of them were locked away in the safehouse and Sofia felt about ready to lose her mind. They weren't being held captive but it was beginning to feel that way. The only bright spots in her days were the guys. She wasn't sure what she would do without either of them, they were quickly becoming her whole world. Sofia was sure she was in love with them both, but she was too much of a chicken to tell them.

Anton's family had been over a few times to visit and she liked getting to know his mother and sister. Every time she saw Valentine's ever expanding belly she longed for a family of her own. Sofia knew it was crazy to hope for something like that with Luca and Ani but she did. Valentine made it look so easy dealing with two alpha men and raising a family along with helping her mother. But a part of Sofia worried the guys wouldn't want any of that with her, which caused her to cautiously guard her heart.

Nick didn't have any updates about her father and Sofia was beginning to feel as though hoping he was still alive was pointless. She wasn't sure how she would feel if Nick's hunch was correct and he was alive and well, living in the witness protection program the Marino family turncoats were placed in. How could she ever forgive him for just leaving her and her mother to fend for themselves. He had to have known they would pay the price for his betrayal and a loving husband and father wouldn't do that to his family.

The raid on the warehouse turned up fruitless. Apparently someone tipped the Marinos off and they were able to move their entire operation. There was no sign of her mother and no news about where they might have moved the women they were keeping in the warehouse to. Sofia had lost hope of ever seeing either of her parents again, even though the guys had tried to stay positive for her. She didn't have the heart to tell them she wasn't holding out the same hope they had.

"Hey," Luca groused. Sofia could tell their self-imposed imprisonment was taking its toll on both of the guys. Luca had put together a makeshift gym in the basement of the house and he and Anton spent a good portion of their day down there. Sofia loved to be able to run on the treadmill while watching her two guys working out shirtless and sweaty. She was quickly finding out a home gym certainly had its perks.

"Hey yourself," she sassed. Luca crossed the room

and plopped down onto the sofa next to her, pulling her onto his lap.

"Ani said his sister and Nick are on their way over," Luca murmured against her neck kissing the sensitive skin behind her ear. They both knew her body inside and out and were always touching and kissing her.

"Well that will be nice," she whispered.

"Yeah," he half-heartedly agreed. Sofia could tell he really didn't mean it though.

"So, why don't you sound very enthusiastic?" she asked.

"I just got off the phone with Mila," he admitted. Luca had kept in contact with his little sister and Sofia even had the chance to speak to her a few times. She apologized for ditching Mila when they were kids and her old friend graciously accepted. Mila also warned her if she hurt Luca she'd personally kick her ass. Sofia knew her friend would do it too, but she couldn't fault her for being overly protective of Luca—she felt the same way about him and Anton.

"Is everything alright with her?" she questioned when Luca didn't fill her in on any details.

"Mila's fine," he said. "It's my father." Luca's voice cracked with emotion and she wrapped her arms around his neck giving him her silent support. "He's, um—he's not doing well. She said if I want to see him again, I should go now."

"Oh Luca, I'm so sorry," Sofia cried. "What can I do to help you?" Sofia knew there was really nothing any of them could do. If they went to Florida they might be walking right into a trap. She wouldn't put it past either family to set Luca up using his father as bait.

"I'm going down to Florida," Luca whispered. He wiped his eyes and Sofia could hear the resolve in his voice. Luca wasn't asking permission to make the trip.

"No, Luca," she begged. "What if the families find you? What if it's just a trap?" she asked.

"She's right," Anton confirmed, standing in the doorway. Judging from the angry scowl on his face he had heard the entire conversation. "You can't just fucking up and go to Florida, man." Luca set her back onto the sofa and stood.

"I have to, Ani. He's my father and I'm his oldest son. This is my duty and I will go to say goodbye to him," Luca said. He stood toe to toe with Ani and Sofia worried they were going to get into a fight. They were both hot heads but Luca's emotions were out of control. She knew if she didn't step in things might get ugly and they would say or do things they would later regret. Sofia stood in between their two big bodies and put a hand on each of their chests. She could feel both of their hearts beating out of control.

"You both need to take a step back and remember you love each other," she said. Her words had both guys stopping dead in their tracks.

"She's right, Luca." Anton sighed. "I do love you and I won't let you just go off and do something that will possibly get you killed." Ani smiled down at her pulling Sofia into his body to kiss her forehead. "Thanks for that, Princess."

Sofia nodded not trusting her words. Hearing Ani tell Luca he loved him made her long to hear those same words from him. Hell, she wanted to hear them from both of her guys, but she was afraid to admit that to either of them.

"You look a little shell shocked, honey," Anton said. "You alright?" Luca crowded up against her other side wrapping an arm around her.

"Ani's right, baby. You look out of sorts. Do you need to sit down?" Luca asked.

"No," she said. "I'm fine," she lied.

"Hmm," Anton hummed. "I think our girl might not be used to hearing me tell you I love you, Luca." Fuck, why did Anton have to be so good at reading her? She didn't want to get into her feelings just before Val and Nick got there. Really, she was afraid to talk about her feelings at all; it was just not something she ever did.

"We will talk more about going to see your father when Nick gets here, babe," Anton promised Luca. "But if you go, then we all go. It's all for one and one for all." Anton chuckled.

"Did you just quote the Three Musketeers?" Luca asked.

"Yep," Anton admitted.

"Thank you," Luca said. "I need to do this, Ani—please understand." Anton nodded and Luca breathed a sigh of relief. "I love you too, Ani. You know that, right?" Luca asked. Anton nodded again and Sofia's heart felt as though it flip-flopped in her chest.

They both looked down at her as if expecting her to go next. All her ability to speak seemed to fly right out the window. Sofia cowardly buried her face in Luca's chest trying to hide from them.

"Knock, knock," Valentine shouted from the back door. She and Nick always came in that way, not wanting to attract any extra attention by going to the front door.

"Hey guys," Nick said. Valentine waddled most of the way into the living room and stopped dead causing Nick to run into the back of her with a humph. "What the hell, honey?" he questioned.

"Sorry, Nick. Would someone like to explain what the two of you did to poor Sofia?" Val asked. Sofia didn't bother to peek out from between the guys still hiding her face against Luca.

"We didn't do anything to her," Anton defended. "We're just waiting her out, hoping that she finally admits she fucking loves us," he growled.

"Well, isn't that something you hope to happen naturally? You know instead of bullying the poor girl for the words?" Val asked. Sofia knew the whole situation was getting way out of hand. She wanted to tell them both she loved them—it was the truth. It was how she felt, but saying those three little words to them scared the crap out of her.

"Can we please table this discussion for another time?" she asked, her face still buried in Luca's shirt. "You know like when we are alone and can talk privately," she added.

"I'm sorry, Sofia," Valentine offered. "I didn't mean to embarrass you." Sofia sighed and release the death grip she had on Luca's shirt, turning to face Val and Nick.

"No, it's not your fault," Sofia said. "You didn't embarrass me. I'm just not very good at admitting my feelings. My family didn't really say those words to each other," she whispered.

"Speaking of your family," Nick interrupted and cleared his throat. Sofia was thankful for the change of topic. "We have good intel your mother is still alive. She is being held at another one of the Marino's warehouses and this time I'm heading up the team who will go in after her." Sofia nodded and covered her sob with her shaking hand.

"Thank you," she cried. "I appreciate that, Nick."

Luca pulled her against his body. "That is great, baby," he whispered into her ear. Anton kissed her forehead and she leaned into him. Sofia was relieved to know her mother might still be alive, but her world felt as though it was still spinning out of control and she was sure it had everything to do with the two big alpha men who held her in their arms. She wasn't sure how she was going to do it but she needed to tell them both how she felt about them. Falling in love was easy; admitting it out loud was proving to be terrifying.

ANTON

They spent the afternoon eating and talking. His mother was watching Val's daughter but she had sent all his favorite foods. He had to admit, he missed his mother's cooking and it felt damn good to have family around again.

"We have another issue," Luca said. Anton wondered how long it would take his guy to bring up wanting to travel to Florida to be with his dad. "My sister, Mila, called to tell me my father's health is failing. She said if I want to say my goodbyes, I should go now." Luca choked up at the mention of having to say his final farewell to his father. Anton knew just how hard it was to lose a parent having lost his dad at such a young age. But he wasn't given the chance to say goodbye or tell his dad he loved him. His father never knew the man Anton had become and he wondered how he would feel about the job he had done so far. He hoped he made decisions that would make his dad proud, especially when it came to protecting his mother and sister. He would do just about anything for his family and that now included Luca and Sofia.

"I don't know if this is a good idea, Luca," Nick said. "It could be a trap and even if it isn't the Gallos, they will have eyes on your parents just in case you show up there. Your entire family is being watched by both the Marinos and the Gallos." Anton knew that would be the case, but he hated that they were putting Luca's family in danger because of what they did. He should have taken Sofia and left Luca out of this whole mess, but Anton also knew he wouldn't be able to walk away from him. Luca owned half his heart and whether or not Sofia wanted to hear it, she held the other half.

"I understand the risk, Nick. I just can't let my father die without telling him goodbye," Luca whispered.

Nick sighed, "I get it man, I really do. I didn't get to say those words to my father and neither did Anton or Val but think about what he would want. Would your dad want you running into a dangerous situation just to see him one last time?" Anton hated the indecision he saw in Luca's eyes. He wished he could make Luca listen to reason but if Nick couldn't talk some sense into him, no one would be able to.

"I need to do this for me," Luca admitted. "Please understand," he said, looking between Sofia and Anton as if pleading with them to just let him go. There would be no way in hell that was going to happen.

"I'm in," Anton agreed. "If you go, I go." Luca

shook his head and Anton expected an argument until Sofia pulled Luca's hand into her own.

"Same," she whispered. "I'm going too." Anton loved how she wanted to be with them both, but he wanted Sofia safe and preferably as far away from any potential danger as possible.

"No," Luca and Anton said in unison. Sofia giggled, which was not the response either of them were expecting.

"There is no fucking way you are going with us," Anton shouted.

Luca nodded and Anton had to admit he was surprised he was actually agreeing with him. "Ani's right, there is no fucking way either of you are going with me. I need to do this on my own. If I had you two with me and something happened to either of you, I'd never forgive myself."

"How do you think we feel, Luca?" Sofia yelled. "You just want to walk away from us and what, waltz right into danger and we're supposed to just let you. We need to do this together, remember? We're the Three Musketeers or have you forgotten that already?"

"No, I haven't forgotten," Luca growled. "I just know I can't lose you or Ani. You're both too important to me."

"Do you think we feel any differently about you, Luca? I fucking love you and losing you would rip my heart out. I'm sure Ani feels the same way," Sofia shouted. Luca shot Anton a look and then smiled like a loon. He had to admit; he knew exactly what the big guy was thinking. Their girl had finally announced she was in love with him, but a part of Anton worried Sofia wouldn't admit to having those same feelings for him.

"Say that again, baby," Luca ordered. Sofia looked around the table at each of their smiling expectant faces as if trying to figure out just what she said. Anton could tell the exact moment she realized what she had done and Sofia closed her eyes, as if wanting to hide from them again.

"How about we give the three of you a little privacy," Valentine offered. Nick stood and pulled her from her chair. "I swear I'm going to need a small crane to help me up for the next few weeks." Valentine rubbed her belly and Nick laughed and kissed her cheek.

"We'll be out back on the porch," Nick offered. "Just let us know when you guys have come to an understanding. Whatever you decide, you will have our full support."

"We love you guys, you're family—all three of you," Valentine said and kissed the top of Anton's head. As soon as Anton heard the back door close he knew Sofia was going to try to change the subject and hide from her feelings. It was her go to move and he hated that she couldn't just share that side of herself with them.

Luca looked determined not to let that happen though. "Did you mean what you just said, honey?" he asked. Sofia hid her face in her hands and groaned.

"We're going to have this out here and now. You might as well accept it, Princess and stop hiding from us," Anton ordered. Sofia let her hands fall from her face and hit the table with a thud. Her expression was almost comical but Anton knew better than to find any of this funny. Too much was at stake now. He wanted to know the three of them had a future together because he couldn't see himself without either of them.

"Fine," she shouted. "You both want to know what I am feeling? I feel you are pushing me out of my comfort zone." Sofia crossed her arms over her chest and sat back in her chair as if challenging them to say another word. Anton stood and pulled her from her seat and wrapped his arms around her. Luca followed his lead and hugged her from behind. They completely encompassed her small frame and there was nowhere for Sofia to hide even if she wanted to.

"How uncomfortable are you now, baby?" Luca whispered against her neck.

Sofia leaned against Luca's body. "This is more like it. I can deal with you touching me. I just never said those words before—to anyone. My parents never really talked about feelings. My mother told me she loved me a handful of times but only on rare occasions. This is all so new for me," she admitted. It made Anton sad Sofia didn't grow up in a warm loving family like he and Val had. It must have been so lonely for her; it broke his heart thinking about Sofia that way.

"I love you, Sofia," Anton whispered. "I don't fucking care if you ever say it back to me because I can see you feel the same way every time you look at me or

Luca. You love us and when you're ready you'll tell us both how you're feeling."

"Thank you," she whispered.

"I love you too, baby," Luca admitted. "I know you feel the same way but I can't wait for you to want to tell me those words again. I won't push you though." Sofia nodded against his chest and he pulled her up his body for a kiss. When Luca finished with her Anton did the same.

"What are we going to do about your father and going to Florida?" she questioned. Anton sighed at the change of subject. They were back to Sofia hiding from them again and they'd let her, for now.

"We're all going," Anton said. When Luca looked as though he wanted to protest, Anton covered Luca's mouth with his hand. "No argument. Sofia was right—one for all and all for one. You go, we go. It's as simple as that," Anton said.

Luca kissed Anton's palm and lowered it from his mouth. "Fine," he groused. "I don't agree with taking the two of you with me but I can't stop either of you from tagging along. But at the first sign of danger you take Sofia and high tail it out of there, got it?" Anton smiled up at him and nodded.

"Let's go tell Nick and get these plans made," Anton ordered. "I don't know about the two of you, but I can't wait to get the hell out of this fucking house."

Sofia giggled, "Same here."

"I'll call Mila and have her tell my mother we are going to be there in the next couple days. I won't give too many specifics just in case, but they need to know we are coming. I'm just hoping we can make it there in time," Luca said. Anton wrapped his arms around Luca's big body and hugged him.

"We will, man. He'll hold on to see you if he knows you are on your way," Anton said. "I'll handle the rest of the plans with Nick. You concentrate on your family." Luca gently kissed Anton's lips and walked up to the bedroom they all shared. Sofia looked torn as to who she should be with. "Go with him," Anton offered. "He needs you now and I'm just going to make arrangements for our flights."

Sofia followed Luca up to their room and Anton worried the three of them weren't going to be able to get down to Florida without some unwanted attention. He just hoped like hell Nick had a good plan because he knew the Gallos and if his hunch was right they would be waiting for Luca to show up to say his goodbyes to his father. Anton would have to do everything in his power not to let them anywhere near Luca or Sofia—it just wasn't an option.

IT TOOK Anton about an hour to plan their trip south and say goodbye to his sister and Nick. They were all set to leave in the morning and he was anxious to get back to Luca and Sofia. They had locked themselves away in their master bedroom to call Luca's sister and hadn't resurfaced since.

Anton opened the door to their bedroom to find Sofia sprawled out on their bed and Luca standing between her legs fucking into her curvy sexy body. "Damn," Anton said as he entered the room. He quickly stripped out of his clothes not needing or waiting for an invitation to join the two of them.

"You two are so fucking hot," he growled. Anton cupped Luca's jaw and kissed his mouth, hard and punishing.

"You taste good, babe," Anton teased, biting and sucking Luca's lips into his mouth. Seeing Sofia and Luca together always turned him on, but tonight he saw the raw carnal desire of Luca's need as he pumped in and out of their woman's body.

Anton got onto the bed with Sofia, the mattress dipping with his weight and gifted her mouth with the same attention he'd just given Luca. He always tried to be gentler with her, but right now his girl was giving as good as he gave. He wanted to mark her, consume her and make her his. Hell, he wanted to do that with them both and tonight and he would.

Anton worked his way down Sofia's sexy body licking and nipping at her sensitive skin. He paid special attention to her gorgeous breasts loving the way he could elicit her throaty groans of pleasure, begging him for more.

"Fuck, Ani," she hissed. "I need more." He flashed her his wolfish grin and snaked his hand down her body to where she and Luca were joined. He cupped Luca's balls driving him to the edge.

"You like that don't you, babe?" Anton teased. Luca pressed his lips together and nodded not able to say the words. Anton leaned forward to kiss his way up Luca's chest and neck keeping a tight grip on his balls while he pumped in and out of Sofia's wet pussy. By the time Anton got to Luca's lips, he was panting with need.

"I'm going to get the lube and fuck your sweet ass, babe," Anton promised. Luca groaned out his pleasure.

"Yes please," Luca hissed. "I want you to fuck my ass." Anton stood from the bed and felt the giddy rush of being with the two people he wanted most—the two people who owned his heart. He loved them both and he hated how Sofia wouldn't give them the words back. But he knew how she felt. He saw it in her eyes every time she looked at him. She loved them both but she was holding back from saying the words. He made a promise to her and Anton planned on keeping it. He wouldn't push her to admit her feelings for them. Neither of them would. She would come to them with her admissions of love, Anton just hoped they didn't have to wait long. He wouldn't hold back from telling either of them what they meant to him. The more Luca and he told Sofia they loved her, the better their chances of her breaking down and admitting her feelings for the them.

"Our guy is going to keep fucking you, baby. I'm going to lube up his ass and fuck him while you milk his cock with that tight pussy of yours." Anton kissed her mouth loving the way she responded to him. "I love you," he whispered against her lips. Sofia looked a cross between panicked and needy causing him to chuckle.

"It's alright, baby. You don't need to give me the words right now. I just wanted to tell you how I'm feeling," Anton said. He rounded the bed running his hands over Luca's sexy muscles mesmerized by the way they bunched and rippled with every thrust into Sofia's body. Anton knew they were both on edge. He would need to move quickly to take Luca's ass.

"I love you too, babe," he whispered against Luca's shoulder. He worked his hand down Luca's back, parting his cheeks to run the pad of his thumb along the seam of Luca's ass. "So fucking hot," Anton murmured.

"I love you Ani, so much," Luca moaned. "Please take my ass and make me yours."

"You don't have to ask me twice, babe," Anton teased. He squirted some lube onto his fingers and worked them into Luca's tight hole. "You are going to feel amazing." Luca thrust back onto Anton's fingers and he couldn't wait any longer. He lubed up his cock and stood behind Luca's big body. Anton was almost as big as Luca but stood an inch or two shorter. He lined his cock up to Luca's tight opening and shoved his way into his guy's ass.

"Fuck yes," Anton hissed. "You feel so good, Luca." The three of them worked in unison to find a rhythm that had him spilling his seed into Luca's ass in no time. He pulled out of Luca wanting to watch him lose himself into Sofia. He could tell she was close and Anton wanted to hear her shout out both of their names as she came. Anton kissed his way down Luca's body to where he and Sofia were joined, licking and sucking her throbbing clit into his mouth. Anton loved watching Luca's cock work in and out of Sofia's drenched pussy and when they both came; he could taste both of their releases on his tongue. It was perfect—they were perfect and his, they were all his.

LUCA

They landed in Florida and Luca felt about ready to burst into flames. He had forgotten how hot and humid it was where his parents chose to live. It was like stepping out into pea soup and a part of him suddenly felt homesick for Chicago. He had pangs of remorse over having to leave his city, but being in the blistering sun and feeling as though Satan had his nuts over a fire slowly roasting them, had him longing for home.

"Wow," Sofia breathed, pulling her long hair from her shoulders up onto her head in a messy bun. "I heard Florida was hot but this is next level," she said.

"Yeah, tell me why people come down here to retire?" Anton complained and took off his jacket. "I'd miss the colder temperatures and snow."

"Oh snow!" Sofia gushed. "Right now I'd give just about anything to be knee deep in snow." Luca laughed at the way the two of them were carrying on. He remembered when his parents moved to Florida and he helped them move into their little condo. Luca felt the same way when he first stepped out of the moving van and into the Florida heat.

"You two will get used to the heat. Besides, we are only going to be here for a few days," Luca said sadly. He hated he was only going to have a short visit with his parents. He needed to remember they were in danger and he should be thankful for any time he got with his dad, especially since it might be the last time Luca might see him.

"I'm sorry, Luca," Sofia said. She linked his arm through his and snuggled into his body. "Here we are complaining like children and you're here to say goodbye to your dad. I wish there was something I could do for you," she said.

"You both being here with me is enough. I don't think I'd be able to get through this without either of you," he admitted. He knew it sounded corny especially since most of his life he had been a loner. But now, Luca couldn't think of one single instance he'd want to go it alone. Not since meeting the two people who completed his heart.

"Well you have us, all of us," Anton promised. "We have your back, no matter what. Just remember—the first sign of trouble and we high tail it out of here," he said. Luca nodded and looked around the small airport for any sign they were being watched or followed but found none.

"Don't worry, Ani. Mila didn't fill my parents in on too many details about our visit, just in case. She told

Ma I was coming down to visit but she wasn't sure when I'd be able to get here. Our trip will be unannounced and will probably be uneventful."

"Well, I'm looking forward to seeing your parents again," Sofia offered. "Do they know about the three of us?" she asked.

"I'm not sure," Luca admitted. He never hid the fact he was bi from his family. But it wasn't something he openly discussed. They had more of a don't ask, don't tell policy when it came to discussing sex. Which was just fine with him. The less he talked about his own sex life with his parents the more comfortable he was. "It depends on if Mila opened her big mouth or not. If you forgot, my little sister likes to spread the news."

Sofia giggled, "Now, that is one thing I do remember about her. You used to tell her she should grow up to be a news reporter with the way she liked to report the news to your parents." Luca chuckled at the memory of his pesky little sister. Mila was always a handful and she knew just how to get under his skin.

"I think that is the car Nick arranged for us," Anton said. He nodded to the black SUV that waited at the valet station. "I'll get the luggage loaded and you grab the keys," he ordered. Luca liked the way Anton seemed to take charge of the trip arranging everything for them so he could concentrate on his visit with his parents. It was the sweetest thing anyone had ever done for him.

It took about thirty minutes to get to his parents'

condo with traffic. He knew they needed to be cautious about just running in and possibly being ambushed, but he was itching to get in to see them both. Anton had him and Sofia wait in the SUV while he ran surveillance of the area making sure no one was watching them. When Ani came back with the all clear Luca breathed a sigh of relief.

"Looks like it's all clear," Anton said. "Ready?"

Luca wanted to tell him he wasn't. He didn't know if he'd ever be ready to tell his father goodbye but he wasn't a coward and he wouldn't run away. Not now—not after they had come so far and risked everything to be there.

Luca texted Mila to open the back door to the condo and his little sister met the three of them on the patio to let them in. Luca pulled his sister in for a bear hug noticing the way Sofia shyly watched them. He knew Sofia felt badly about how her relationship ended with Mila, but he hoped they had been able to move past all of that the few times they spoke on the phone recently.

"Sofia," Mila gushed, wrapping an arm around her old friend. "I'm so glad you came with him." Sofia nodded. "Two years is way too long to have to go without seeing you, big brother."

"Well, if my little sister wasn't so determined to leave her family and run all the way to California we might see each other more," Luca teased. He saw the sadness in Mila's eyes and he knew he had unintendedly hit a sore subject.

"How is your dad?" Sofia asked. Mila shook her head unable to speak past her sob. Luca pulled his little sister into his arms. He wished he could fix this for his family but there was nothing he could do. As the oldest and the only son, he was going to need to step up and be the head of the household. He wondered how he was going to fill his father's shoes while running from the two largest mafia families in Chicago.

Mila pulled free from his hold and smiled up at Ani. "You must be Anton," she guessed.

"Yes," he said. Anton pulled Mila in for a quick hug. "Luca has told me so much about you. I can see why my brother can't keep his hands to himself," she sassed. Mila had always been bold even as a child, but watching her give Anton a little guff made Luca chuckle. Anton turned a cute shade of pink and Luca thought it was the sexiest thing he'd ever seen.

"Um, thanks," Ani murmured.

"Are they awake? Can I see him?" Luca interrupted. He loved how Mila was taking the time to get to know the two most important people in his life but Luca was ready to see his father.

"Yes," Mila said. "They are in the master bedroom. Mom hasn't left his side this whole time."

"We'll be right here, man. If you need us, just yell," Anton said. Sofia pulled him in for a quick hug and released him.

Luca nodded and turned to walk to the back of the condo where his parent's bedroom was. He lightly tapped on the door and heard his mother's soft voice tell him to come in. He hesitated as if trying to decide if this was what he really wanted to do. He had always known his dad to be a strong capable man. Seeing him beaten down by dementia wasn't the way Luca wanted to remember him. He had to do this, more for his family than himself. Luca needed to be by his mother's side and help her through all the upcoming trials even if it was uncomfortable for him. He owed both of his parents that much.

Luca pushed open the door and smiled at his mother. She stood from her bedside chair and slowly made her way to Luca as if she wasn't sure it was him or not. "Hi, Ma," Luca choked. She wiped the tears from her eyes and wrapped her arms around his waist.

"My Luca," she whispered. "You've come."

"Always, Ma," he promised.

"We just thought—with everything going on." He knew his situation with the family must have been hard on his parents, especially his father. Stanley Gallo was a staunch family supporter. He believed once you were in you were in for life and he served the Gallo family until Luca was old enough to take his place. This whole mess with Luca going against the family had to have been a difficult pill for his father to swallow. Luca worried he would have disappointed his parents and that would have broken his heart. He never intended to hurt anyone. Luca just couldn't blindly follow orders anymore and overlook everyone who was trapped in the family's crossfire.

"Nothing could keep me away, Ma. He's my

father," Luca said. It was hard to speak around the lump in his throat. Luca looked past his mother to where his father was resting and almost didn't recognize him. The disease had taken its toll on his dad's mind and body over the past year.

"How is he doing?" Luca asked, although he could see his answer for himself.

"Not well. The doctors said it could be any time now. They wanted him to go back to that awful hospital but he wanted to be at home in his own bed." His mother looked back at her husband and Luca could see the pain behind her smile. "He's a proud strong man, Luca. You're a lot like him."

"Thanks Ma, but I'm not feeling very strong right now," he admitted. "Why don't you let me sit with him for a while? I brought two people who I want you to meet. You know Sofia Marino from when she used to come to the house to play with Mila?" His mother smiled and nodded.

"She used to follow you around like a lost puppy," his mother teased. "It's so sad what happened to her family." Luca didn't want to get into what happened to Sofia's family. He had a feeling his mother might feel the same way as his father would about the subject. If you went against the family you took your punishment. They would see what happened to Sofia and her mother as collateral damage for what Mr. Marino chose to do to them. Where he saw shades of grey his parents saw only black and white.

"Anton is here too," Luca whispered, changing the subject.

"Well, I've been looking forward to meeting your partner. We knew his parents too. His father worked for the Gallos around the same time as Stanley," she said.

"Listen Ma, I'm with them," Luca said. From the confused look on his mother's face Luca knew he was going to have to spell it out for his mother and that was a conversation he really didn't want to have right now. He never hid who he was and he wasn't about to start now.

"With them?" she questioned.

"Yes, with them, Ma. I'm in love with them both and they love me. We're happy—the three of us," he said with a shrug. Angela Gallo wasn't a hard woman and he knew she would want only happiness for her only son. At least that was what he was hoping. It seemed to take her a minute to process what he was telling her, but as soon as she worked it all out his mom smiled up at him, patting his chest.

"You have a good heart, Luca. They are both lucky to have you," she said. He dramatically exhaled causing his mother to giggle. "Always such a worrier, son. I've always known who you are. You're my first born and my only boy. Nothing will change how much I love you, Luca," she whispered.

"Thanks, Ma," he said, his voice gruff with emotion. "Go take a break and I'll sit with Dad." His mother nodded and left the room. He smiled at the hushed voices that floated down the hall as Mila made introductions. He imagined his mother pulling both Sofia and Anton in for bear hugs and that thought made him happy.

"You made it?" Luca wasn't sure if he was imagining his father's whispered question or if he was really awake.

"Yeah Dad, I made it." Luca went to his father's bedside and bent to kiss his father's cheek.

"I was worried you wouldn't get here in time," his father said. He looked Luca over and he wasn't sure if he was feeling love or scrutiny in his dad's gaze. He was probably just tired and overly sensitive about their whole trip.

"How long will you be here?" his father asked. Luca hesitated in telling him the plans Anton and Nick made. He knew he should be able to trust his own father but what if he was wrong? He could be landing all three of them in danger and that thought had him rethinking his answer.

"Just a day or so," he said, keeping his answer simple.

"Good, good," his father said, closing his eyes as if it was just too much for him to stay awake.

"Get some rest, Dad. I'll be here when you wake up again and we can talk then," Luca offered.

"Fine," his father whispered. "Go be with your mother," he ordered. "No sense in you sitting here watching an old man sleep."

"I'll check back in on you soon," Luca agreed. "Get

some rest." His father seemed to fall to sleep before Luca even left the room and he quietly shut the door behind him, following the sound of Sofia and Mila's giggles to the kitchen. Luca was looking forward to a few days' visit with his mother and sister. He needed to help them make plans to properly say goodbye to his father. Then, Anton, Sofia and he would need to find a new place to lay low for a while. Luca was starting to feel this mess with the families was never going to disappear and he wondered if he was going to spend the rest of his life looking over his shoulder or if the three of them would find some small piece of happiness away from the only lives they ever knew.

SOFIA

Sofia sat on Anton's lap as they watched Luca and Mila reminisce about their father and she had to admit she felt a sadness she'd since forgotten. Losing her father was tainted by her own worry after he betrayed the Marinos. She and her mother barely had time to grieve for him before the family showed up to take their pound of flesh. They were never given a body to bury and her mother had opted for a small memorial to remember her father. Not many attended the service for fear of retribution from the Marinos. Sofia's mother told her to move on and forget him as if her entire world hadn't just crumbled to the ground. She wasn't close to her father, but his death left several unknown variables she had to worry about daily. The Marinos were good at waiting for their prey to drop their guard. She thought she was safe and even found herself relaxing into a daily routine again when they showed up outside her gym and shoved her into their van. Sofia worried the same thing would happen to the three of them now. The families would wait for them to become comfortable, giving them a false sense of security and then they would swoop in and destroy everything the three of them had built together.

"You were such a brat," Luca teased his sister. Mila didn't seem to mind her brother's assessment.

"Well, being the youngest had its perks," she agreed. "But when you all left me I wasn't quite sure what to do with myself." Mila shot Sofia a sad look making her feel bad for the way she had left things between the two of them. Sure, they had a few conversations by phone, but Sofia wasn't sure the hurt feelings were all cleared up as Mila had promised her.

"It wasn't her fault," Luca defended, picking up on the sudden friction between the two of them. "Sofia was just a kid and she was probably as lonely as you were. Besides, who could blame her for falling for me?" Luca flexed his muscles, making them all laugh. He was so good at diffusing tense situations. Sofia wasn't sure what she had done to deserve him or Anton but she wasn't about to question her luck.

"I am sorry, Mila," Sofia said. She stood from Anton's arms and crossed the small family room to where Luca and Mila sat on the sofa together. Luca pulled her down onto his lap and she willingly let him.

"I know, Sofia," Mila whispered. "It's just that seeing you now with my brother after all these years— well, it's just a little surreal. I guess it just makes me miss you and our friendship." Mila reached for Sofia's hand, holding it in her own. "I'd like for us to be friends again, Sofia."

Sofia's heart felt about ready to burst. She quickly nodded her head, "I'd love that, Mila."

"Good. I figure since you love my brother and all, we should at least go shopping or have lunch," Mila teased. Sofia felt panicked at the mention of the "L" word again. They had just been through all this the day before, with Nick and Valentine front and center to witness her awkward denial of feelings about the two men who held her heart. Now, she was going to have to experience all the uncomfortable stares as she worked through this new wave of denial.

Anton and Luca's amused expressions told Sofia all she needed to know—they were going to be of no help. "Um," Sofia squeaked.

"It's alright, baby," Luca murmured. "We don't need to get into all of that again. Anton and I already told you we can wait until you are ready." She hated she was being a complete chicken. Honestly, she was ready to tell them she loved them. She had been for weeks now, but every time she tried to get those words out they seemed to get stuck in her throat and she looked like a fool.

"Oh, I'm sorry," Mila floundered. "I didn't know you weren't to that point in your relationship. If I overstepped, I'm sorry."

"It's fine," Sofia offered, trying to sooth her old friend. The last thing she wanted to do was make Mila feel uncomfortable.

"Our Sofia hasn't admitted she loves us yet. Well, unless you count the one time she mistakenly said she loved Luca," Anton said. His tone was teasing but Sofia heard the undertones of his sadness and even hurt. She hated she was doing that to him. Anton was just as much a part of her as Luca was. Did he honestly believe she wasn't in love with him too? Of course, the fact she refused to give either of them the words didn't help her case.

"Who's hungry?" Angela Gallo stood in the doorway, wooden spoon in hand and Sofia wanted to kiss the woman for her perfect timing. From the smirk on the older woman's face, she had heard the gist of the conversation and knew exactly what she was doing by interrupting.

"I'm starving, Ma," Luca admitted. "We missed lunch and I've missed your cooking," he said.

They spent most of the evening sitting around the table eating and laughing and Sofia wasn't sure if her life had ever felt so normal. Her parents never really had family dinners except for when his father entertained other family members. Her mother hated the whole cooking and cleaning scene and being part of a traditional Italian family wasn't something that came easy for her. Sofia had to admit she felt the same way about many of their traditions, but the thought of being barefoot and pregnant cooking for her two guys did crazy things to her heart. She wanted to take care of them and even though she always swore otherwise, she wanted kids—lots of them. She had always been so lonely as an only child. Sofia could see herself with a family like Luca's with kids going in and out, driving her crazy. It sounded just about perfect to her. But, she was jumping ahead of herself. First, she needed to tell the guys she loved them. Not giving them the words was starting to hurt them both and that was the very last thing she wanted.

"Hey, where did you just go?" Anton whispered to her. Luca watched the two of them from across the table and she smiled at his intense stare. They were always watching her, touching her and making sure she was all right. It was time she started doing the same for them.

"I was just thinking about the future," she admitted. "What our dinner table will look like and who will be sitting around it." Anton's face lit up as if he had caught onto her meaning.

"Do you want kids, Sofia?" Mila asked. Sofia swallowed and nodded.

"It's crazy but I do. I never thought I'd ever want to have kids," Sofia said. Luca's eyes were still on her and she worried she had crossed a line admitting something so private with his mother and sister in the room. They hadn't even discussed what they were going to do past tomorrow. Especially now with everything so up in the air. Sofia worried Luca wasn't ready to talk about a future involving her, Ani and kids.

"Sorry," she murmured. "We can just talk about this later."

"I like that you want to have kids, Sofia," Luca said.

"I want a houseful." Anton took her hand into his and squeezed her fingers with his own.

"Me too, Sofia," Anton admitted. Sofia nodded, suddenly unsure of herself.

"I'm going to check on Stanley," Mrs. Gallo said, standing from her seat. Anton and Luca stood to help her clear the dishes from the table.

"Here Ma, I've got this. I'll go and check on Dad and you relax," Luca ordered.

"Such a good boy," Mrs. Gallo gushed, patting his arm. "Thank you, Luca." He carried the dishes to the kitchen and on his way back to his father's room, pulled Sofia into his arms to gently kiss into her mouth.

"We aren't finished talking about those kids you want, honey. As soon as we get to the hotel I plan on doing some practicing," Luca teased. Sofia playfully swatted at him and shooed him down the hallway. Her guys were going to be a handful, especially if she could follow through with her plans to tell them just how much she loved them tonight. Sofia was sure they'd never let her out of bed again after she admitted those three little words to them.

ANTON

Anton was beginning to worry about Luca. He had gone to check on his father over an hour earlier and he wondered if his guy had fallen asleep on the chair next to his father's bed. Anton wanted to get Sofia and Luca to the hotel and hash out a few things before stripping them both bare.

"I'm going to go back and check on Luca," Anton said. He kissed the top of Sofia's head and stood to make his way back to the bedroom.

"Please Dad, don't do this." Luca's pleading voice bled through the door and everyone of Anton's defenses went up. "There has to be another way here, guys," Luca insisted.

Anton carefully pressed his ear against the bedroom door, trying to figure out what was going on. If his hunch was correct, Luca and Mr. Gallo weren't alone in the bedroom. "You don't get to decide what is best for this family yet, Luca. I'm still alive," Mr. Gallo coughed.

"I understand that Dad, but this isn't the answer either. I'm supposed to just go with them and then what?" Anton wanted to burst into the room at the mention of Luca going anywhere without him. Whoever was in the room with the two Gallo men, they were there for a purpose and Anton was sure it was to take Luca back to Chicago. He couldn't allow that to happen. He wouldn't let anyone take Luca away from him or Sofia. Still, he needed to be smart about things and getting their girl and Luca's family out was the first thing he needed to do. Anton pulled his cell from his pocket and shot off a quick text to Sofia. It was short and sweet and he just hoped like hell his message to "Get out now", would be enough to have her moving her curvy little ass out of the house and taking Luca's mom and sister with her.

"It's time to go," a man's voice said. Anton knew he needed to make his move or chance losing the man he loved.

Anton pulled his gun from his shoulder holster and pushed the bedroom door open. "He's not going anywhere with you two," Anton shouted. He looked around the room, surveilling that his quick body count was correct. Two men stood in the corner of the room by a door he assumed led to the back patio and the probable way they gained entrance.

"Drop the guns and kick them over to me," he ordered. They both did as he told them and Anton looked them both over. He didn't know either man but that didn't mean anything. The Gallo organization was large enough he wouldn't know everyone, even with his role as Isabella's right hand man. A part of him wondered who Isabella found to replace him after he disobeyed her and took off with Luca and Sofia.

"I take it Isabella sent you?" Anton questioned. He watched the men carefully, waiting for them to make any sudden movement.

"My father called them," Luca growled. Anton had to admit; he wasn't really surprised. He and Nick planned for something like this—he just hated they needed a plan for Luca's father betraying them.

"Why?" he asked.

Mr. Gallo coughed and wheezed, "Because my son betrayed the family—again," he spat. "I had to, Luca. I won't let your mistakes hurt your sisters or mother." Anton saw the hurt and betrayal on Luca's face and he knew both emotions would have to play out. He just needed to keep it together long enough to get him and Luca out of there, but knowing his guy he was going to give hm a fight about leaving his father.

"I taught you everything you know and this is how you thank me? You were given everything and you just threw it away," Mr. Gallo shouted. Anton could tell there would be no talking to him. Mr. Gallo was old school and set in his ways. Anton knew his only hope was to get through to Luca and get him out of there.

"I couldn't turn a blind eye anymore, Dad. You would have me forget my integrity and just follow orders? That's you, Dad. It's not me," Luca said. "But turning me over to the Gallos isn't the answer."

Out of the corner of his eye Anton noticed one of the guys backing slowly to the back patio door. "Not another move asshole," Anton warned. "We need to get out of here, Luca. Sofia knows what to do, we need to stick with the plan," he ordered. Anton trained his gun on the two goons in the corner of the room and said a prayer Luca would listen to reason. They each had a part to play and Anton was beginning to worry Luca would forget his.

"You leave here, Gallo and she won't stop coming for you," one of the guys growled. "You either, Rossi," he promised.

"We'll take our chances," Anton assured. "We need to go now," he said to Luca.

"I can't just leave him," Luca said, looking down at his father. "He might have ratted me out but I can't just leave him here alone with them."

"If you stay here with him you won't be able to protect me or Sofia. You will be gone and then where will we be? We can't lose you," Anton all but whispered.

"You can't keep running, son. Sooner or later, they will catch up with you and if that fails they will go after your sisters or your mother. Do you want that?" Mr. Gallo asked. Anton worried he wasn't going to be able to convince Luca to leave with him, but he knew them both staying there wouldn't end well.

"Luca," Sofia's soft voice startled Anton and he cursed.

"I thought I told you to get the fuck out of here?" Anton shouted.

"I did," she said. "Luca's mom and sister are safe but I couldn't leave you guys. All for one and one for all," she said.

"Fuck," Anton cursed. He hated the way she used their words against them.

"No, Sofia," Luca scolded. "You can't fucking be here. You need to stick to the plan and let Ani and I handle all of this."

"What plan are you two going on about?" the second guy asked. Anton knew Nick's plan was risky, but his gut was screaming at him that Luca's father would betray him—and ultimately them all.

When he and Nick sat and planned out their trip, his brother-in-law was smart enough to put a contingency plan in effect just in case things went sideways. "You didn't think we'd come in cold did you?" Anton asked the two morons who stood with their hands in the air in the corner of the room.

"Luca?" Mr. Gallo questioned. Luca looked down at his father, his smile mean and nodded.

"Yeah," Luca admitted. "Anton planned for everything even my own father betraying me."

"I'm sorry, Luca," Anton said. "I didn't want to be right." Sofia's sob reminded him she was still in the room. "Get behind me, honey," he ordered.

When he heard Luca and Mr. Gallo weren't alone

in the room he texted Sofia to get the hell out of the house, but he also sent a text to Nick who had followed them down to Florida. When his brother-in-law proposed he follow them down south to watch their backs, Anton thought he had lost his mind. He was sure Nick was just being overzealous in his protection of the three of them, never imagining Luca's own father would rat him out to the Gallos. Sofia was supposed to get Mrs. Gallo and Mila to safety and wait for the two of them at the hotel. If they didn't show up by morning she was supposed to head to Mexico and disappear. Instead their girl jumped right into the fire with them and Anton wasn't sure how he felt about it. He wondered if she'd ever obey either of them, but he was pretty sure he already knew the answer. Sofia was a handful and that was the way they both liked her. It's what drew them to her.

Within minutes the condo was swarming with agents and detectives from the local police department. "Good job, Ani," Nick praised as he strode into the bedroom. "We can take it from here."

Anton holstered his gun and pulled Sofia around his body and into his arms. "Are you ever going to listen?" he chided. She gave him a shy sexy smile and shook her head.

"You can't do this," Mr. Gallo protested. "He has to pay for what he did. It's the only way to keep my girls safe," he pleaded. Anton felt badly for the older man; he really did. He knew just how Mr. Gallo felt. He would have done anything to make sure Luca and Sofia were safe. Hell, he traded his own life to keep his mother and sister's family out of the Gallo organization. But he saw what his father's betrayal did to Luca and the sadness in his eyes nearly did Anton in.

"You should have trusted me to keep my sisters and mother safe, Dad. I wouldn't ever let anything touch them but turning myself over to the Gallos isn't the answer. We plan on bringing down the family and we will too, our way. The old ways are dying and sooner or later good will win out." Luca crossed the room and wrapped his arms around Anton and Sofia and Ani's world felt right again.

"You're wrong," Mr. Gallo protested. "Isabella Gallo will never concede. She will find a way to destroy us all."

"Not if we destroy her first," Luca growled.

AFTER THEY GOT DONE ANSWERING the local authorities questions, Nick helped to find them a safe place to stay for the night. Anton worried things with Luca's father weren't going to change and he hated that Luca's last memory with his father would be such a hateful one.

Luca climbed into bed with Anton and Sofia, fresh from the shower and pulled them both into his big body, as if needing the comfort. "When do we leave?"

"You know you can go back and talk to him tomorrow, right?" Sofia questioned.

"Yeah, I know. I just have nothing left to say to him," Luca admitted. "I told Ma and Mila I'd be in touch when we figure out our next move. I just can't face him again."

Anton sighed. He knew all too well living with betrayal and disappointment wasn't a good combination. "Don't let things end this way with your father. Take it from two people who didn't have a choice in whether we got to say goodbye. Go to him and make things right. Hell, at least say your peace and get everything off your chest. If you don't you'll regret it later."

Luca nodded and cuddled into Anton's side. "I'll think about it. Can we just get some shut-eye?" Anton knew there would be no more talk about forgiveness and betrayal tonight. When Luca was tired he shut down and his guy had to be emotionally exhausted from everything that happened.

"A good night's sleep sounds perfect," Sofia said around a yawn. She stretched and cuddled into Anton's other side.

"Fine, but we pick up this discussion in the morning," he said. Anton worried he was going to get the same answer but he didn't want to push. Luca forgiving his dad before it was too late was too important.

LUCA

Luca woke early and tried to quietly rummage through his luggage to find some workout clothes. He needed to go for a run to work out some of the demons that plagued him all night. He had a fitful night of tossing and turning and Luca worried he kept Sofia and Ani up along with him.

He quickly dressed and left them a note he was going for a run. Luca didn't really care if he might still be in danger or that going out wasn't the best idea. He needed to clear his head and running always helped do that for him. He started out not really knowing where he was going just aimlessly running to forget. But before long he realized he was headed straight back to his parent's condo. He wasn't sure if it was the dumbest thing he'd ever done and frankly, he didn't care. Anton was right, he needed to get a few things off his chest and set things straight between him and his dad.

Otherwise, they might never find a path forward and that thought scared him.

Luca gently knocked on the back door not wanting to cause a scene or wake his entire family. It was still early and his sister was not a morning person. Mila used to give him hell when he woke her to drive her to school.

"Luca," Mila opened the door and yawned. "You know how I feel about early morning wake-up calls," she grumbled.

"I know," he whispered. He didn't apologize. There would be no use—he wasn't really sorry. This was something he had to do and he could see Mila understood that.

"Come in," she offered. He brushed past her and stood in the foyer not sure what his next move would be. He hadn't really planned any of this and he suddenly wished Ani and Sofia were with him. They were his rocks, his sounding boards and his voices of reason.

"You look a little lost," Mila murmured.

"I feel it," he admitted. "I'm not sure what I'm doing here," he said.

"You are a good man, Luca. You're here because despite how wrong our father was in trying to turn you over to the Gallos, you want to forgive him. He was trying to protect the rest of us, but what he doesn't understand is we wouldn't want anything to happen to you just to save our own asses."

"I appreciate that, Sis," Luca murmured, pulling her in for a quick hug. "Give me a minute with him."

"Ma is in the kitchen making coffee. I'll be in there," Mila offered. Luca nodded and started towards his parents' bedroom. He needed to say his peace and get back to Ani and Sofia before they worried about him.

Luca quietly pushed the door open to find his father peacefully sleeping. He looked around the room as if expecting to find the chaos from the night before. His dad peeped an eye open and Luca knew there would be no turning back.

"Hey," Luca whispered.

"You came back?" his dad asked.

"Yeah. I couldn't leave without saying goodbye to Ma and Mila," Luca said. He knew he sounded angry but he had every right to be.

"I did what I thought was right, Luca," his father whispered. "I'd do it again to keep your mother and sisters safe," he admitted. Hearing that his father didn't regret turning him over to the very family that wanted to kill him hurt. How could any father want to cause his child any pain or suffering? Luca was sure he'd experience that and so much more at the hands of the Gallos.

"I understand wanting to keep them all safe," Luca said. "It's why I've been working with Ani's brother-in-law, Nick and the NYPD. We are trying to bring down the Gallos and the Marinos and we will, it's just going to take some time." Luca's father shook his head as if silently disagreeing with him.

"It will never happen, son. Better men than you have tried and failed," his father choked. Anton's father and even Sofia's father were casualties of the family's combined efforts to weed out moles and destroy them.

"We won't fail, Dad; it's not an option. My family is too important to me. The family that Ani, Sofia and I are going to build together is worth the fight," Luca said. He knew they had a lot of obstacles to overcome but he needed to try. For the first time in his life Luca had something worth fighting for and he wouldn't back down now.

"I hope you're right son; I really do. Just promise me one thing—you will take care of your sisters and mother." His father's voice cracked and Luca knew exactly what was being asked of him. He would always protect them, no matter what.

"Always," Luca whispered. He turned to leave knowing he wasn't going to get what he had come for. He and his father were both too proud or maybe even too stubborn to come to a crossroads. He was going to walk away from his father knowing he had his integrity even if he didn't have his father's trust. If he had that, his father would have never had to have asked him to promise to protect his family. His dad should have known him well enough to know that was a given.

SOFIA

Nick found them a quaint little house in upstate New York and Sofia had to admit it was just about perfect. She never realized places like these existed in the state. When she was growing up she foolishly believed New York, much like Chicago, was all city. Sofia was pleasantly surprised to find the world was a much bigger place than she ever imagined and she was enjoying discovering them all with her two guys.

It had been over a month since they left Luca's family in Florida. Just days after they left Luca got the call from Mila that his father had passed. She and Ani offered to go to the funeral with him but Luca insisted he wasn't going. He told them it would only put his mother and sister in danger and he wouldn't do that to them. Mrs. Gallo had her husband's body flown back up to Chicago to have him buried in the family plot and according to Mila all the major families sent representatives to pay their respects. Luca and Ani believed they were there to watch for the three of them to make an appearance. Sofia was just glad they were tucked away, safe from the drama of mafia families and loyalties that were so often betrayed.

Sofia's biggest issue was how she was going to tell the guys that somehow, in the midst of all of their chaos, she had gotten herself pregnant. When they got settled in their new safe house she started to suspect something was off. She was sick most mornings, moody and couldn't turn off her emotions. Every little thing seemed to set her off and she blew it off as being under too much stress. When she finally realized she might be pregnant, she snuck out to buy a pregnancy test only to have her fears confirmed. If her calculations were correct she had just over five months to tell the guys and with the way she was being a coward about sharing her news, that might be cutting it close. Sofia wished she had someone to talk to but she knew she couldn't tell Mila. Her old friend would blab to Luca and that wasn't what she needed right now. She missed her mother. At least her mom would have some idea of how to tell the guys they were about to be daddies.

"Nick is on his way here, baby," Anton said, stepping into the bathroom where she was soaking in a tub. "He's about ten minutes out and he says he has some news about your mother." Sofia nodded, not able to speak past the lump of emotion in her throat.

"Got it. Thanks," she croaked.

"No baby, don't cry," Anton soothed. "You've been so on edge lately. What can I do to help you?" She choked back her laugh at the irony of it all. There was nothing he or Luca could do to help her. She was the one who had gotten pregnant and had kept it to herself for weeks now. The longer she let the news fester, the more it seemed to grow and plant seeds of self-doubt inside of her. Sofia wanted to believe they would both be happy about the baby but she honestly didn't know.

"I'm fine," she said, waving him off. "I just need a few minutes to pull myself together, please." Ani nodded and turned to leave.

"You know you can tell us anything right, honey?" Sofia sniffled and nodded.

"Yes. Thank you, Anton. I just have a lot on my mind. I'll be fine," she lied. Sofia watched as Anton left the bathroom and wondered if she had just made a huge mistake. He'd given her an opening and she brushed it off. If she was going to spill her news she wanted to tell them together.

After her bath, Sofia could tell that Nick had showed up and was in their kitchen. Her only clue he had arrived were the hushed whispers that filtered down the hallway to their bedroom where she finished getting dressed. Sofia knew they just wanted to protect her but she was stronger than they gave her credit for. If Nick had news about her mother she was going to have to get her shit together and face it head on like she did everything in life.

She made her way down the hall trying to make as much noise as possible to alert the guys she was coming. "We just need to tell her," Luca insisted.

Sofia leaned against the doorframe, "Luca's right," she said. "You should definitely tell me what's going on with my mother." She crossed her arms over her chest and didn't miss the way Ani or Luca looked her over. "None of that now guys," she chided. Nick laughed and she shot him a look that told him she wasn't amused.

"Right," he said. "We have news about your parents."

"My parents?" Sofia asked. "I thought you were here about my mother?" Nick had been by with weekly updates about her mom, usually to tell her that they had no news. There was no mention of her father since they first arrived. She knew Nick believed her father somehow made it out of the Marino organization and escaped to New York but she couldn't bring herself to accept it as a possibility. The idea of her father leaving her and her mother to face the Marinos on their own was almost too much to believe.

"Your father has been found. He's been in the NYPD witness protection program until he's called to testify. He was one of the men who were lucky enough to get out, with a handful of others," Nick said. "He wants to see you, Sofia."

Luca made his way over to where she stood and seemed to hesitate. "It's alright if you don't want to see him, honey," Luca whispered. Ani framed her other side and she felt completely surrounded by the two men she loved most in the world.

"I just don't know what I want," she admitted. "I'll have to think about it, if that's alright?" Nick nodded.

"Your mother was extracted from a Marino warehouse this past weekend. I didn't want to tell you until I had confirmation. She's been through a lot, Sofia. They have her in a hospital and she's safe but she has asked for no visitors." Sofia nodded her understanding.

"Not even me?" Sofia whispered.

"I'm sorry, no. She doesn't want to see anyone right now, Sofia. Your mother has been through so much, just give her time to come around," Nick said.

"Will she be alright?" Sofia asked.

"She's pretty banged up and has a couple broken bones but they think she will make a full recovery," Nick said. Sofia felt a relief she hadn't felt in some time. Knowing her mother had made it out of the hell they were in despite her father walking away from them gave her some peace. She just hoped that someday her mother would want to see her again. They had never been very close but she wanted to see for herself her mom was safe.

"I do have some good news to share with the three of you." Nick seemed to perk up and Sofia was hopeful he had news on their proposed truce with the families. After they returned from Florida, Anton met with Isabella again, but this time she came to him. Isabella wasn't pleased about having to fly to New York for their meeting but he left her no alternative. He also set up a meeting with the head of the Marino family, under the same conditions. Nick and Ani planned on getting the two families in the same room and laying their cards on the table. Luca reluctantly stayed home with Sofia after Ani made him promise to protect her—no matter what. The meeting went as well as they could hope for, but no real decisions were made and Sofia worried they'd have to stay in hiding forever.

"Let's have it," Anton ordered.

"Both families have agreed to back off. You three are free as long as you steer clear of either families business," Nick said.

"So letting both sides know we had enough evidence to bring them down worked?" Luca questioned. During the meeting, Nick and Ani basically told both the Gallos and Marinos between the three of them, Sofia, Luca and Anton had enough hard evidence to build a case to bring both of the families to their knees. In exchange for their and their future family's freedom they had to agree to take their evidence to their graves. Sofia knew Anton and Nick hated they were so close to demolishing the two families and couldn't use their intel to bring them down. But she also knew Ani would do just about anything to keep her and Luca safe.

"Yeah. It sucks we won't be able to shut both sides down, but you three are free and that's all that really matters." Nick shrugged. "It's the least I could do for you, Ani. He did the same for my family and I'll forever be grateful."

Anton nodded at Nick, "They're my family too, Nick. You all are. We take care of family," Ani said.

Nick stood, "Think about seeing your father, Sofia. Life is too short to hold grudges. Next time I come up this way I'll bring Val and Ace. We are dying for you all to meet our new little guy. Maria misses you guys too." Nick pulled Sofia in for a quick hug and watched as Anton walked him out.

Sofia saw how Anton's face seemed to light up at the mention of his niece and new nephew. She knew both her guys would accept her pregnancy and Nick was right—life was too short for grudges and secrets.

Luca wrapped his arms around her waist. "You don't have to see him you know. You can take your time and think about what you want—what your next move will be."

"You went to see your father," Sofia reminded him.

"Right, but that was before I knew he was going to turn me over to the Gallos. It was before he put your and Ani's lives in danger. If I had known my father was going to hand me over to the family I wouldn't have gone. Things weren't good between the two of us when I left him. But I said what I needed to say and I've made my peace with the whole situation. You just have to find your peaceful solution and Ani and I will respect any decision you make." Luca kissed the top of her head and she leaned into his body. For such a big man he had his moments of tenderness and she loved him for it.

It was time for Sofia to tell them everything—all of it and let the chips fall where they may. She knew her guys wouldn't let her down but that still didn't make saying everything aloud any easier.

Anton came back into the house and stood in front of her. He dipped his head to gently kiss her lips. "You alright, honey?"

"Well, let's recap," she sassed. "I have a father who is supposed to be dead, wanting to see me. I have a mother in the hospital who refuses to let me visit." Sofia sighed and snuggled into their bodies. "No, I'm not alright," she sobbed. Sofia hated she was crying once again. It seemed to be all she did lately.

"Talk to us, honey. Tell Ani and I what we can do," Luca pleaded.

"You know if it is something we can help you with, we will," Anton agreed.

"You can't help me with this. It's something I just need to either accept or not. I can't change who my parents are. They have never been the warm loving parents you both seemed to have. I grew up very much alone and often afraid." Anton tried to interrupt her and she held up her shaking hand, effectively stopping him.

"I just need to get this out, Ani." He nodded and pulled her hand to his mouth, kissing her fingers. Sofia smiled up at him and shook her head. "Don't try to distract me either," she giggled.

"Sorry." He smiled but she could see he was anything but sorry.

"As I was saying," she said without any real heat. "I had a lonely childhood and the two people who were supposed to protect me were busy with their own personal objectives. I don't think I will ever be able to forget what my father did to my mother and me. He got out of the family and I'm happy for that, but he left the two of us to face his consequences. What type of man does that to his family?" She looked Luca and Ani up and down, as if sizing them up. Neither of them would ever do that to her or their kids. They were both honorable, decent men and the thought of either of them walking away from her to save their own asses was laughable.

"You two would never do that to me or our baby," she assessed.

"Thank you for that," Anton said.

"Wait- our baby?" Luca questioned. Sofia didn't try to hide her smile. She was done being a coward. It was time to tell her guys just how she felt about each of them.

"Yes," she whispered. "I'm pregnant."

"When did you find out, Sofia?" Anton questioned.

"I started to suspect things after we came back from Florida. I've known for a few weeks now," she admitted.

"And you didn't think to tell either of us we are going to be fathers?" Luca demanded. This was not going the way she planned and Sofia worried she had blown things with them by not telling them earlier.

"I'm fucking this all up," she sobbed. "I'm sorry I didn't tell you—either of you, but I was scared. I'm not scared anymore and I'm ready."

"Ready for what?" Anton asked. She could see the question in his eyes and maybe there was some hope too but Sofia didn't want to get ahead of herself.

"I'm ready to tell you both I love you," she admitted. Luca and Anton stood side by side in front of her and they both gifted her with their sexy smiles. They already knew how she felt about them; they weren't blind. She had been in love with them both for months now.

"We know, baby," Luca teased.

"We've known for a while now. It's just nice to hear you say the words, Princess," Anton said.

"You have both been so patient with me and I don't know what I would have done if you would have pushed me to say those words earlier." Sofia laughed. She knew exactly what she would have done. Sofia would have run as far and as fast as possible in the other direction had they pushed. But they were both so kind and loving, patiently waiting for her to admit what they had to have seen in her eyes every time she looked at them. She was in love with them.

"And we're having a baby?" Luca asked. She could hear the hopefulness in his voice and she giggled.

"Yes. If my calculations are correct you will be daddies in about five months." Anton picked her up spinning around with her, causing Sofia to squeal. "Put me down, Ani. I don't want to be sick."

"You've made us both so happy, honey," Anton admitted. He dipped his head down and took her lips in a gentle kiss. She loved how her big alpha man could be so gentle.

"I love you, Ani," she whispered against his lips.

"Love you too, baby—both of you," Anton said, reaching for Luca's hand.

"My turn," Luca said. He pulled Sofia up his body and kissed his way into her mouth. His kiss was hard and demanding and she wouldn't want him any other way.

"I love you, Luca," she said panting from his kiss.

"I love you too, Sofia. I love both of you," Luca said. He pulled Anton against her back sandwiching her between their two bodies and Sofia finally felt as though she found her home, her future—her forever.

ANTON

Two months later

Anton helped Sofia into her coat. He had to admit he'd fallen in love with upstate New York and after Nick gave them the all clear two months back, he worked night and day to convince Luca and Sofia they had found their home. He was thankful it didn't take too much coaxing to get them to go house hunting with him. He was ready to put down roots and raise their growing family in a place that felt safe and finally free of their past baggage.

"You look beautiful, baby," Anton offered. He ran his hands over her expanding belly and she belted out her laugh.

"You do like my bump, don't you, Ani?" she teased. The truth of it was he did. Both he and Luca couldn't seem to get enough of her belly. Seeing her pregnant with their child did crazy things to his heart. Anton never imagined he could be so happy. He always thought being bisexual meant he would have to sacrifice a part of himself to have a normal life. He never thought he could have everything he wanted in needed but he had found that with Luca and Sofia.

"We both do, honey," Luca teased palming her belly. "You're sexy as fuck, but seeing you pregnant makes us both a little crazy," he admitted.

"How about we just get through today and then you both can show me just how sexy you find me," she promised. As far as plans went, Anton had to admit it sounded like a good one. He worried she might change her tune though after the exhausting day they were about to have.

"You'll let us know if you can't handle this, right honey?" Luca asked. Sofia smiled up at them both and it just about took Anton's breath away. He could tell this whole ordeal with her parents had weighed on Sofia. Her mother had remained adamant she didn't want to see her daughter. Sofia worried she had done something to upset or even anger her mother and Anton found the whole notion ridiculous. If anyone should be pissed off about what happened, it should be his girl. Her parents failed her and he couldn't figure out why they would do that to Sofia. She was the kindest, gentlest woman he had ever met. As a soon to be father he could never imagine any scenario that would make him put his wife or child in danger as Sofia's father had.

"I will," she promised. Sofia went up on her tiptoes

and gently brushed her lips against his, repeating the same sweet gesture with Luca. "I love the way you both take care of us," she said rubbing her belly. "I love you both, so much."

"Us too, baby. We'll always take care of you and our little one," Luca said, covering her hand with his own. "You are our entire world," he promised.

"Well, how about you help your entire world out to the SUV. It might take both of you to hoist me up into that seat." Sofia giggled. "I swear I haven't seen my toes in weeks now," she teased.

"If it makes you feel any better they are still there, Princess," Anton joked. Sofia stuck her tongue out at him and he wondered how long they'd be able to keep up the facade that everything was alright. They were about to meet the man who walked away from Sofia and her mother, leaving them both in danger. If it were up to Anton he would never allow his girl to meet with her father. In his book, her dad was a monster who didn't deserve a second chance, but many people might feel the same way about him. Anton knew what he did for the sake of family business. He knew he didn't always do the right thing—hell, he knew he wasn't a good guy, but he was thankful as fuck Luca and Sofia both gave him a second chance.

Nick set up the private meeting for Sofia, after she agreed to meet with her father. He was still under witness protection with the NYPD until he could testify and Anton was happy the meeting was close to their home. He knew traveling too far was starting to get harder for Sofia. It had taken her a couple months to get to this point and honestly, he never thought she would agree. Sofia flip flopped between wanting to meet with her father to tell him off and wanting to see him to tell him she forgave him. Anton didn't think the man deserved either.

"You know you don't have to do this, Princess," Anton said as they pulled up to the address Nick had sent him. The tiny house stood dark and quiet. To the unsuspecting eye it looked as if no one was home. But Anton noticed the undercover detectives that surrounded the place. He hated they were potentially walking their girl into danger.

"I know, Ani. I need to do this for our and our baby's futures." Anton nodded, knowing there would be no talking her out of this meeting—he and Luca had both tried. Sofia was the most stubborn woman he knew and talking her out of what she wanted usually ended up with him and Luca both giving into her anyway.

"We have your back, baby," Luca promised. He got out of the SUV and helped Sofia out. Anton flanked her other side and they went into the house. Nick met them at the door and nodded to Sofia.

"You ready to do this?" Nick questioned.

"As ready as I will ever be," Sofia admitted. "Where is he?" she whispered. Anton hated the hint of apprehension he heard in her voice. Their girl was usually so confident and strong, he knew this meeting was taking its toll on her.

"He's in the kitchen," Nick said reaching for Sofia's hand. "You don't have to do this, you know." Anton loved the way his family had accepted both Sofia and Luca into their lives. Valentine loved Sofia as if she was a true sister and all the guys got along famously. Anton couldn't have dreamed of the merging of their families to go any better.

"Why do all of you guys keep saying that to me?" Sofia asked. "I'm going to be fine. I'm here to say my peace and then we can leave."

Anton pulled her against his body. "Then let's do this. If I remember correctly Luca and I have something we need to show you when we get home," he teased. Sofia's blush was adorable as Nick ushered her through the house to the small kitchen.

Vincent Marino sat at the big table that took up most of the kitchen, standing when he saw his daughter walk into the room. "Sofia," he said, smiling at her as if no time had passed. Mr. Marino seemed to be treating the whole meeting as a casual reunion and Anton knew Sofia felt anything but casual about seeing her father again.

"Dad," Sofia didn't put on any fake pretenses, her usual beautiful smile absent from her sober face. "You look well."

Vincent nodded and Sofia made no move to join him at the table. Luca and Anton flanked her sides and she reached for both of their hands, as if needing their silent support. "You look beautiful, Sofia," he said. "I see you're going to be a mother. Who's the father?" he asked, looking between Anton and Luca. He hated that their relationship was any of her father's business. Vincent Marino walked away from his family and in Anton's opinion he lost the right to ask his daughter any personal questions.

Sofia's smile was mean and didn't touch her eyes. Anton could tell she was just as pissed as he was about the question. "The baby is Luca and Ani's," she admitted. "Not that my relationship is any of your business Dad, but I'm with both of them." They both wrapped a protective arm around her waist.

"You don't seem very happy about our reunion, Princess," Vincent accused. "Why agree to meet with me if you don't want to?"

"I thought it would be a good idea to get a few things off my chest. I don't want to bring my daughter into this world with any negativity in my life. I owe my child at least that much. I want her to have my full attention. She shouldn't accept anything less from me," she spat. Anton was so fucking proud his girl didn't back down from her father, but he worried this was all too much for her and the baby.

"You alright, honey?" Luca whispered for just them to hear.

"Yes, thank you," she said, smiling up at him.

"How about we sit down and you can tell me just what you've come to say. But, I hope you'll give me the same courtesy, Sofia," Vincent motioned to an empty chair across the table from where he sat. Sofia seemed reluctant at first but finally conceded and took a seat.

Anton and Luca sat on either side of her still holding her hands.

"Okay, Dad. Why don't you go first?" Sofia offered.

"I appreciate that, Princess," he said. "First, let me say I'm sorry I put you and your mother in an uncomfortable position. That was never my intent."

Anton could feel the anger rolling off Sofia and he knew she wouldn't be able to hold back from telling her father just how his decision to walk away from them affected her. Sofia laughed, "Uncomfortable position, Daddy? After you left I was abducted by the Marino family and sold off as a virgin bride in their meat market. The only reason I'm alive and safe today is because Ani and Luca bought me. I'd hardly call that an uncomfortable position."

"Right," Vincent said, "But you got out and from the looks of it, you're happy. Hell, you might even look at this whole mess as me helping you find happiness." Luca stood, his chair scraped against the kitchen floor and his expression was murderous.

"What the fuck is wrong with you? Sofia was humiliated and held against her will. She and her mother were treated like animals and you are taking credit for her happiness? Anton and I are the reason for Sofia's happiness—you didn't have a fucking thing to do with it." Sofia gently tugged Luca's hand trying to coax him to sit back down with her.

"Thank you, Luca," she murmured.

"You never have to thank me for sticking up for

you, baby. I won't sit here and listen to this bullshit," Luca growled.

"I'm not trying to insult you or what you've been through, Sofia," Vincent amended. "I'm just saying I'd like another chance. Don't you believe in second chances?"

"Sure I do, Dad but this isn't your second chance. I've forgiven you time and time again. You were never there for me, ever. Why now? You faked your death and walked away from Mom and me. You left us without a second thought or look backwards. What changed?" she asked.

Vincent sighed, "I've had a lot of time to reflect on my life while I've been under witness protection," he said. "I want to be in your life and possibly your mother's again someday."

"That's laughable, Dad. Do you have any idea what Mom has been through?" Sofia questioned.

"No," he admitted. "She refuses to see or talk to me."

"Well, at least we have that in common. My mother won't have any contact with me. But I refused to just accept that so I did a little digging and found out what she went through. I needed to know why my own mother wouldn't agree to see me." Sofia paused and shot Luca and Anton an apologetic look. Neither of them had any clue she had dug for answers. Anton had a feeling his brother-in-law had a hand in helping her, but he couldn't be angry with Sofia for needing answers or at Nick for helping her.

"Sorry guys but I had to know," she whispered.

"It's fine, honey. We'll talk about it later," Anton offered. Sofia nodded and returned her attention to her father.

"My mother went through hell after I left," she sobbed. Luca wrapped an arm around her shoulder and pulled her into his chest.

"It's okay baby, take your time," Luca said.

Sofia took a deep breath, "I'm fine, really," she promised them both. "My mother paid the price for us both," she said to her father. "First, you left and she had to give up her life. Mom was a prisoner in the same warehouse as me. They locked her away like an animal and every time I acted out, they threatened to rape her since they weren't allowed to tarnish the virgin bride."

"What happened after we left with you?" Luca asked.

"After I snuck out of Chicago with the two of you the family made good on their threats. From what I've heard from Nick, they kept her in a cage and used her until she had nothing more to give," her voice broke and Anton had just about enough of this family reunion.

"Honey, this can't be good for the baby," Anton warned.

"We're fine. Besides, I'm just about finished here," she promised.

"We haven't reached a resolution," Vincent growled.

"We probably never will, Dad and I'm fine with that," Sofia said. "I made peace with my loneliness months ago. Meeting Ani and Luca showed me what true love looks like. You never loved anyone but yourself, did you Dad?" Sofia didn't wait for her father to give her an answer. Anton could tell she really didn't want one.

"I hope you can find your own peace with what you have done to me and my mother. But your forgiveness from me doesn't come with a free pass to hurt me again. I can't let you back into my life and be a good mother to this baby. I won't let you hurt me ever again." Anton stood and helped Sofia from her seat and Luca joined them to leave.

"You didn't come here intending to forgive me," Vincent accused. "You came here to spew accusations and say your peace, but listening to me was never on your agenda."

Sofia smiled back over her shoulder, "Well, I am my father's daughter, aren't I?" she asked. Luca flanked her back and they ushered her to their waiting SUV. Sofia pulled Nick in for a quick hug and thanked him.

They were about halfway home before any of them dared to speak. Watching Sofia fiercely stand up for herself wasn't a surprise. Their girl was fierce and seeing her in action this afternoon was just confirmation.

"You were fantastic," Luca whispered, kissing her forehead as she leaned into him.

Anton pulled her against his own body gently kissing her mouth. "I love you, Sofia," he said.

"I love you both too. Thank you for being there for me today," Sofia said.

"Always," Anton promised. "We'll always have your back."

"You two are my world and now, we can move forward and I'm so grateful you two stumbled into that auction," she said.

"Going against orders and buying you was the best decision we've ever made," Anton teased. He held Sofia and Luca in his arms feeling like the luckiest guy in the world. Anton had finally found his happiness and he would never let blurred lines tear him away from either of them again.

EPILOGUE

MILA

One Year Later

Mila Gallo watched the moving truck pull away and shut the front door to her mother's new townhome. If felt strange being back in Chicago without her father or brother. Luca promised to visit as soon as Zia was old enough to appreciate traveling. Mila's ten month old niece was the cutest little girl and as her Godmother, Mila couldn't wait to spoil her rotten. But, when it came to getting on a plane her Goddaughter threw quite a tantrum and Luca wasn't ready to endure another non-stop scream fest to visit them.

    Mila knew it was more than just a cranky baby holding Luca back from visiting Chicago. Her brother lived with the demons of his tainted past with one of the largest mafia families in the city. Having the same last name that personally linked them to the Gallo family was a burden they all learned to carry. Her older sisters married and had taken their husband's names, helping them to hide in plain sight. Mila had to admit she wasn't quite ready to settle down and at just twenty-three, why should she be?

When she was called down to Florida to say goodbye to her dying father, she made a promise to her brother she would honor their mother's wishes and take her back to Chicago to live. Mila really had nothing keeping her out in California, where she lived alone and really had no friends to speak of. Her job, working in a local daycare, was the only bright spot of her days and if she was being honest, she was looking for any excuse to move back home. Chicago might have come with the challenges of everyone knowing her family's mafia links but it was where most of her friends and family was. Moving home meant she'd be closer to her sisters and their kids. It meant her mother would be able to build stronger bonds with her grandchildren. It also meant she'd have to see her ex-boyfriend Maxen Fontana. Max was more than just her ex; he was her first love. Hell, he was Mila's only love and the main reason she ran to California as soon as she turned eighteen.

"Mila," her mother called from the back kitchen. The townhome her mother bought was homey and perfect for her. It was one story and Mila wouldn't have to worry about her mom having to climb steps. It was also close to shopping and within walking distance to most of her mother's friends. Mila's plan was to stay with her mother for a few weeks and then find a place of her own. She was used to being on her own and even though her mother insisted she was welcome to stay with her; it wasn't what either of them needed. Her mom was going to have to learn to be on her own for the first time in her life and Mila knew that had to scare her mom to death. Her mother was old school Italian, moving directly from her parents' home to her new husband's. Losing the patriarch of the family was going to be rough on all them, but Mila worried it was going to have the biggest impact on her mom. She was her husband's best friend, wife and in the end, caregiver. Being on her own was going to be touch and go for Angela Gallo, but Mila didn't know a stronger, more capable woman. Her mom was her hero and Mila knew she would be just fine.

Mila walked back through the townhome to the kitchen and found her mother elbow deep in a packing box, trying to lift a stand mixer that weighed more than she was capable of lifting. Her face was red from exertion and her long gray hair was pulling loose from her messy bun. "Jesus, Mary and Joseph, Ma. You don't need to do that. I told you I'll help." Mila shouted. She pulled the stand mixer from her mother's shaking arms and set it on the countertop.

Angela plopped down in the nearest kitchen chair and pushed her unruly curls from her face. "I just wanted to get this mess cleaned up," she admitted. Mila looked around the room at the mountains of moving boxes and burst into a fit of giggles. Her mother didn't look one bit amused by her outburst.

"The moving truck literally just pulled away and this 'mess' as you so lightly call it, will take days to get unpacked and put away," Mila said between giggles.

"Honestly Mila, you could show me some respect. I'm still your mother and you shouldn't make fun of me." Her mother tried to sound upset, but Mila knew her mom well enough to hear the undertones of amusement in her voice.

"Sorry, Ma," she sassed. "How about I start unpacking the kitchen and you find the bed sheets and make the beds. The movers put everything together for us already. Then, I'll take you out for a nice dinner at Maria's?" Her mother perked up at the mention of her favorite restaurant. Mila had to admit she used to love going there as a kid. They had the best baked ziti she had ever eaten and the thought of it made her mouth water.

"Now that, my precious baby girl, sounds like the best idea I've heard in a long time," her mother said. She stood and made her way through the mass of packing paper that laid strewn across the kitchen floor to pull Mila in for a tight squeeze. She missed those hugs when she lived in California and being back home with her mother just felt right.

Her mother started out of the kitchen, a new pep in her step with the promise of dinner and Mila almost wanted to laugh again. "Oh, Ma," Mila called. "Don't forget I have a job interview tomorrow. The nanny agency said they found a family I'd be a perfect fit for." Angela nodded and smiled, turning back to go find the bedding. Mila left out the part about the family requiring a live-in nanny for their two children. She knew her mother would put up a fuss about the two of them having just moved back home together. Every time she brought up finding her own place her mother quickly shut her down. Mila had a feeling she'd feel the same way about having to live with another family full time. Her mom would probably give her an earful about them being strangers and it just not being right for a young girl to live with people she barely knew. It was similar to the same speech she gave Mila when she announced she was moving to California. It was the same day her parents announced they were moving to Florida to retire. Mila saw her opening and she jumped at it. At least then her mother had her father to take care of and dote on. This time, she only had Mila and she had a feeling moving out would be a challenge. Mila decided she'd share when she had news. Until then, she just needed to get through this job interview and wow the potential new family tomorrow because her bank account was dwindling and she had no other prospects. She was starting over and desperate—not a winning combination.

MAXEN

Max Fontana loved his job, if that's what he could call being the new owner of Maria's Italian Family Restaurant. When he heard about the business going up for sale he jumped at the opportunity to follow his lifelong dream of owning a restaurant. He made the owner an offer that was probably above market price but he didn't care. He didn't want to take any chances with his favorite place to eat in all of Chicago. He grew up going to Maria's and now he would make sure future generations would grow up enjoying the best Italian food in the city. He had his dream job and a very empty bank account to show for his efforts—but he was happy, for the most part.

His mother liked to give him hell about not settling down yet, but at twenty-eight he had other dreams and goals. He had plenty of time before he needed to find a good Italian woman to settle down with and have babies, as his mother liked to say. He needed to manage one part of his life at a time and right now, his restaurant came first. Women were a nice distraction and he enjoyed spending time with them, but he never quite found the one he'd wanted to settle down with. He let that one walk away and he knew finding another woman like Mila Gallo would take time. Hell, it would be damn near impossible to do, but that was his own stupid fault for letting her go.

Max was lucky enough to keep most of the staff after he took over the restaurant and that included the same chef who had been there for the past twenty years. He counted himself lucky that, for the most part, he had people working for him he knew and trusted. It made the transition much smoother for the change in ownership. Max knew he needed to learn the ins and outs of every part of his business and tonight, besides making his rounds asking if everyone was having a good time, he was going to play host. Seating people was always a major challenge since the regulars liked to have their special booth and were often not willing to sit just anywhere. Tonight was no exception. Maria's was packed and he had at least a thirty minute wait for parties of four or more.

"Hi," a familiar voice said. Max had his back turned to the woman but just her voice had his heart racing. "Do you have a long wait for a table for two?" He knew Mila's voice before he even turned around to face her. "Oh," she stammered, seeming caught off guard.

"Hi Mila," he all but whispered. "I didn't know you were in town." Mila looked him up and down and smiled.

"I've moved back with Ma," she said.

"Yeah, I was sorry to hear about your father. My condolences," he said to Mrs. Gallo. Mila's mother stood behind her daughter and from the look on her face, running into him wasn't a part of her plan. Mila's mother wasn't always his biggest fan, but after things fell apart between the two of them, Mr. and Mrs. Gallo froze him out completely.

"Thank you, Maxen," Mrs. Gallo said dryly. "Do you work here now?" she asked. He could feel Mila's eyes on him and he wanted to ask her if she was staying in the city or if she was going back to California. God, he wanted to ask her to be his again but he had no fucking right.

"I own the place," he said, looking at Mila. "I bought it a few months back." Mila's smile was back in place but it didn't touch her eyes. Max waited for her to say something—anything—but she didn't.

"How nice," Mrs. Gallo said. "Do you have a table for two available for Mila and me?" Mila looked around the room at all the pictures that adorned the walls; pictures he knew like the back of his hand.

"You didn't change anything, did you?" Mila asked. Max shook his head not trusting his voice. She was so beautiful with her long dark hair pulled back into a messy bun. She wasn't wearing much make-up, but she never really needed any. Her trademark red lipstick still turned him completely on, making him want to taste her lips and more. But he lost that right with Mila a long time ago.

"No," he said. "This place means too much to me to change anything," Max admitted. "We had our first date here," he almost whispered.

"Yes and you asked me to marry you in that corner booth when I was just fourteen," she said, smiling at the memory. "And I told you yes," she whispered. He remembered the day as if it was just yesterday. He was almost eighteen at the time and had just met the most beautiful girl he'd ever laid eyes on—Mila. Her father and brother, Luca both warned him to stay away from her, but he couldn't seem to bring himself to do that. He didn't care if she was a few years younger than he was, he fell in love with her at first sight and there was no going back. Max wished he could turn back time and go back to tell that kid not to fuck things up with the only woman he'd ever love but that wasn't possible. He couldn't love her enough to change who he was for her. He never be able to admit to her she wouldn't ever be enough for him.

"You look good, Mila," he said.

"Thanks, you too Max," she murmured. He almost had to lean into her body just to hear her, but Mila took a step back and it felt as though she physically slapped him. "I'm sure you have customers to get back to," she said changing the subject.

"Of course," he said. "I'll show you and your mother to a table." He led the way back to the family room reserved for his VIP customers and helped both women into their seats. "Enjoy your dinner ladies." Max smiled and walked away. It's what he was good at, his go to move and one that still hurt like hell.

GABE

Gabriel Leone helped his five year old son look under his bed for the one shoe which always seemed to elude them when it came time to leave each morning for school. They were always ten minutes late and he was starting to wonder if he'd ever be on time for anything ever again. Gabe had gotten good at being both mother and father for his son, Michael and his daughter, three year old Gia. He had no choice but to be everything they both needed since losing his wife three years prior, just after she gave birth to Gia. His beloved Angel gave him two precious gifts and he'd forever be grateful even when he was on his hands and knees, pulling piles of dirty, stinky boy clothes from under the twin bed while looking for one missing shoe.

"How come I have to go to school?" Michael asked. "Gia gets to go play all day and I wanna do that too," his son protested. They had this conversation at least every other day and it always ended the same way—with both of his kids wrapped around his legs, crying and begging him not to leave them. Gabe had no choice though. He had a job to do and as the police commissioner of Chicago, an important one at that.

"We've been over this before, Michael. You have to go to school because it's the law and I'm the head of all the city's police men and women. How would it look if I broke the law? They wouldn't let me do my job and catch the bad guys anymore," Gabe said, trying to reason with his son. Michael's scowl told him he wasn't buying his explanation.

"It's just not fair," Michael pouted.

"I know, son but it's what us big guys have to do. We have responsibilities now, you and me." His son's scowl turned into just a grumpy shrug and Gabe took it as a win. "How about you go and get your sister and meet me in the kitchen. I'll make us some breakfast and we can walk to school today." Michael seemed to perk up at the mention of walking to school. His kids both loved to be outside and Gabe had to admit, it was a pretty great way to start the day with sunshine and fresh air.

After a quick breakfast, he triumphantly held up Michael's shoe he found in the dirty clothes hamper and helped Gia on with her shoes. They were going to actually make it to school on time this morning and he was starting to feel pretty good about the whole single parenting thing.

Gabe pulled open his front door just as a pretty brunette held up her hand to knock. "Oh," she said. "I'm sorry. I must have the wrong address. I'm looking for the Leone family."

Gabe looked her up and down, "I'm sorry, but do I know you?" he asked.

"So, I have the right address then?" she questioned.

"Well, I am Gabe Leone, if that helps," he offered. The woman seemed a little flustered by his admission.

"I'm your eight o'clock appointment for the nanny position," she said, holding her hand out to shake his.

He took her hand into his and tried to wrack his brain about making an appointment for the morning. "I'm sorry, I don't remember having an appointment this morning," he admitted.

"Oh, well maybe your wife made it?" she questioned. Gabe looked down to where Michael fidgeted with his jacket. He didn't really remember his mother, but any mention of her always seemed to upset him.

"I'm not—" Gabe stammered. "She's not—I'm not married."

"Oh sorry," she offered. "I received a call from the nanny agency I'm signed with and they told me to be here at eight. If this isn't a good time—" Gabe knew his assistant had probably set up the meeting for him. Jules was always doing things like that for him and not telling him. He couldn't fault her since she was his older sister and just looking out for him. Still, he needed to remind her to put all his meetings on his calendar, even ones she thought might piss him off. Honestly, a nanny wasn't a bad idea. He knew he couldn't keep juggling everything life was throwing at him and keep his new job as commissioner.

"I'm sorry, what's your name?" he asked.

"I'm Mila Gallo," she said, smiling up at him. She was really lovely but much too young for him. Besides, he wasn't interested in dating right now. His current status involved secret hook-ups which usually led to hot, casual sex with men he met at local bars. He kept that part of his life as private as possible though, especially since he was the city's commissioner. Admitting he was bisexual wasn't something that won the people's trust, unfortunately. So, he kept his sex life under wraps, on the down low—it wasn't anyone's business who he slept with.

"Um, I hate to do this to you, Miss Gallo is it? As in Chicago's Gallo family?" Mila's smile faded at the question of her last name and he worried he hit a nerve. He knew the Gallo family personally. Hell, he had put many of the family members behind bars.

"Yes," she murmured. "But my family isn't involved with them anymore," she admitted. "My brother got out and is living in New York now and my father passed." Gabe hated how he made her feel as though she had to explain her family to him.

Gabe nodded, "Understood," he said. "Listen, I have to walk my son to school and then drop Gia at daycare. You are welcome to walk with us and we can talk on the way."

"Okay," Mila smiled.

"I'm Gia," his daughter piped up and took Mila's hand to step off the front porch. I'm this many," she said, holding up two fingers. Gabe chuckled at his daughter. She hadn't quite mastered the art of holding up three fingers when telling people how old she was.

"No sweetheart," he corrected. "You are this many," he said, holding up three fingers. Gia looked down at her own fingers and frowned, working on trying to make her hand look like his. "It's alright baby you'll get it," he promised and took Michael's hand in his own. His son was just at the age where he still liked to hold his father's hand and give him kisses and hugs when they got to school but Gabe knew that wouldn't last much longer.

"This is Michael," Gabe introduced. His son was a little shyer than his outgoing daughter and Gabe knew when to push and when to stand back and let Michael take the lead. He really didn't do well with strangers and Gabe knew this whole situation had to be pushing him deeper into his shell. Michael was placed in therapy after Angel died and he never seemed to outgrow the need to see his therapist every other week. That was just fine with Gabe, he'd do whatever he had to to insure his son was happy and healthy. He knew his son had some issues he needed to work out and his therapy sessions really helped.

"Hi Michael," Mila said. His son smiled up at her and nodded.

"He's a little shy," Gabe whispered and she giggled.

"That's okay. I was shy too, when I was your age. I'm the youngest of seven kids and I never really seemed to fit in, no matter how hard I tried."

Michael nodded again. "I like soccer," he whispered.

"Hey, I played soccer in high school," Mila said. Gabe scooped Gia up, carrying her ahead, to give his son and Mila some time to get to know each other. If Jules had her way, he'd be hiring a nanny today and Mila seemed as good a fit as any, especially if the kids approved of her.

When they got to Michael's school he asked Mila if she could help him with shooting goals after school. When she looked up at Gabe, not knowing how to answer Michael's question, he smiled and nodded.

"Mila and I have a few more things to go over, but I'm sure you will be seeing her again soon," he promised. His son's face lit up and he had to admit, Jules was right about getting a nanny. Not that he'd ever admit it to her. Telling his older sister she was right about anything usually ended poorly for him. She could gloat for days if he allowed it.

"Thank you," Mila said. "I appreciate you giving me the chance. I just moved back to the area with my mom and I am afraid I'm starting all over again."

"I'm sorry. You said your father passed?" Mila nodded and he instantly regretted his question.

"About a year ago," she offered. "My mother wanted to come home to Chicago and I have to admit I did too. When I turned eighteen, I moved to California but I hated it. I was going to go to college, but I'm twenty-three now and I'm thinking it might be too late for that."

"Nonsense," Gabe said. "You're still so young. You can do anything ,really. Wait until you get to be my age then you'll really be stuck in your ways."

Mila giggled again and he thought it was the sweetest sound he had heard in a long time. "You don't look very old and set in your ways," she rebutted.

"Thanks for that. I just turned thirty-three and I have to admit, I feel more like I'm eighty-three most days. I guess that's why my sister, who is also my assistant, went behind my back and called a nanny agency for me.

"If this isn't what you want," she said, holding up her hands in defense.

"No," he said, shutting her down. "It's exactly what I need. I just hate having to tell my sister she was right," he groused.

"I get it. I have four older sisters and I don't think I've ever admitted that to any of them," she said, making a face that made him chuckle. Gabe wasn't sure of the last time he had a more pleasant conversation or laughed so much in one morning.

"This is Gia's daycare. Why don't you come in with me and meet her teachers? That way when you start—

um, tomorrow, if that works for you—they will already know who you are."

Mila smiled up at him and nodded. "Tomorrow works," she agreed. "Thank you Mr. Leone," she said.

"Gabe," he offered. "Call me Gabe."

To be continued in Ties That Bind book 3!
The End

ABOUT THE AUTHOR

About K.L. Ramsey

Romance Rebel fighting for Happily Ever After!

K. L. Ramsey currently resides in West Virginia (Go Mountaineers!). In her spare time, she likes to read romance novels, go to WVU football games and attend book club (aka-drink wine) with girlfriends.

K. L. enjoys writing Contemporary Romance, Erotic Romance, and Sexy Ménage! She loves to write strong, capable women and bossy, hot as hell alphas, who fall ass over tea kettle for them. And of course, her stories always have a happy ending.

ABOUT THE AUTHOR

K.L. Ramsey's social media links:

Facebook
https://www.facebook.com/kl.ramsey.58
(OR)
https://www.facebook.com/k.l.ramseyauthor/

Twitter
https://twitter.com/KLRamsey5

Instagram
https://www.instagram.com/itsprivate2/

Pinterest
https://www.pinterest.com/klramsey6234/

Goodreads
https://www.goodreads.com/author/show/17733274.K_L_Ramsey

Book Bub

https://www.bookbub.com/profile/k-l-ramsey

Amazon.com
https://www.amazon.com/K.L.-Ramsey/e/B0799P6JGJ/

Ramsey's Rebels
https://www.facebook.com/groups/ramseysrebels/

Website
https://klramsey.wixsite.com/mysite

KL Ramsey ARC Team
https://www.facebook.com/groups/klramseyarcteam/

KL Ramsey Street Team
https://www.facebook.com/groups/ramseyrebelsstreetteam/

Newsletter
https://mailchi.mp/4e73ed1b04b9/authorklramsey

ALSO BY KL RAMSEY

The Relinquished Series

Love Times Infinity

Love's Patient Journey

Love's Design

Love's Promise

Harvest Ridge Series

Worth The Wait

The Christmas Wedding

Line of Fire

Torn Devotion

Fighting for Justice

Last First Kiss Series

Theirs to Keep

Theirs to Love

Theirs to Have

Theirs to Take

Second Chance Summer Series

True North

The Wrong Mr. Right

Ties That Bind Series

Saving Valentine

Blurred Lines

Coming Soon:

Taken Series

Double Bossed

Double Crossed

Made in the USA
Middletown, DE
29 July 2019